Real Mermaids

DON'T WEAR TOE RINGS

Real Mermaids
DON'T WEAR TOE RINGS

HÉLÈNE BOUDREAU

SCHOLASTIC INC.
New York Toronto London Auckland
Sydney Mexico City New Delhi Hong Kong

ISBN 978-0-545-43636-6

Copyright © 2010 by Hélène Boudreau.
Cover and internal design copyright © 2010 by Sourcebooks, Inc.
Cover design by JenniferJackman.com.
Digital illustration by JenniferJackman.com.
All rights reserved. Published by Scholastic Inc., 557 Broadway,
New York, NY 10012, by arrangement with Sourcebooks
Jabberwocky, an imprint of Sourcebooks, Inc. SCHOLASTIC
and associated logos are trademarks and/or registered
trademarks of Scholastic Inc.

12 11 10 9 8 7 6 5 4 3 2 1   11 12 13 14 15 16/0

Printed in the U.S.A.   40

First Scholastic printing, December 2011

For Lauren, who always laughs in all the right places

"Just keep swimming."

—*Finding Nemo*

Chapter One

I BOLTED UPRIGHT IN THE bathtub and hacked a mouthful of water. A wave sloshed onto the tile floor.

"Jade?" Dad's knock sounded from the other side of the bathroom door. "You okay, honey?"

"Yea…yeah," I managed to say between coughs, embarrassed that I'd fallen asleep in the tub, freaked out that I must have slipped underwater. I took a long, shaky breath. "I'm fine, Dad. Thanks."

A shiver ran along my damp arm as I pulled a strand of hair from my mouth. What would have happened if I hadn't woken up? My thoughts turned instantly to Mom.

No. I couldn't go there…

"Can I get you anything?" Dad asked.

I rubbed my eyes and instantly regretted it. Epsom salt. Tear ducts. Ye-owch. Real smooth, Jade. But at least the cramps were gone.

"No, I'm good." I blinked through the haze to the counter where Dad's drugstore bag spilled over with Super Maxi

32-packs and extra-long panty liners. Hadn't I tortured the poor guy enough for one day?

"Call if you need me." Dad's footsteps moved away from the door and continued down the hall.

"I will."

But I wouldn't. I shouldn't.

Yes, getting my first period was a big deal, but I was almost fourteen, for crying out loud. I didn't need to run to daddy every time I had a puberty crisis. It had been a year since Mom drowned; it was time for me to start figuring things out on my own. Dad had enough to deal with.

Dim light from the streetlamp shone through the pebbled glass of the bathroom window. My eyes burned, plus my legs had gone numb and felt like they'd been set in a block of cement. It was late. I should get dried off, head to bed, and finally put an end to this cruddy day.

I braced my hands on the side of the tub and shook my legs to get the blood flowing, but the sight that broke through the foamy surface of the water made me forget the pep talk I'd just given myself about not bothering…

"Dad!"

The world tipped on its axis as I worked to make sense of what I was seeing. I blinked, trying to focus. What the heck had happened while I'd been asleep? Was I having some kind of allergic reaction to Epsom salt? Had someone slipped hallucinogenic drugs into that Slurpee at the mall?

Those and other crazy thoughts shuffled through my brain as I struggled to understand why, instead of legs, the lower half of my body was now encased in a shimmering tail of iridescent scales.

"Ohmigod! Dad!!" I shrank back against the tub, disgusted by what I saw, but the tail moved with me. A sharp breath threw me into another fit of coughing. I shook my head.

Hard.

Dad's footsteps clattered along the wooden floor in the hall.

"What is it?" His voice rang through the door.

"Call 911!" The words escaped between coughs.

The knob rattled. "Unlock the door, Jade! Let me in!"

I tried to haul myself over the side of the tub to stretch my hand toward the door, but my lower half flickered uselessly in the water.

"I can't…"

Dad jiggled something in the lock, no doubt one of his trillion Swiss Army knife attachments, but it proved useless judging by the curse words he muttered. Finally, he rammed his weight against the door. A rush of air filled the room as the door flew open and slammed against the wall.

I pulled a towel to my chest from the towel bar above the tub as Dad stumbled into the bathroom.

"Look!" I lifted the tail from the water and struggled to catch my breath.

Dad's whole body jerked as he took in the blue-green scales shining from the tail. He collapsed onto the toilet seat and leaned heavily against the vanity.

"Do something!" I wailed.

Dad sat, frozen in place. He stared, mouth open, at my half-girl, half-fish body. After what seemed like forever, he spoke.

"Oh, Jade…I'm so sorry…" He ran a hand through his hair. "Your mom and I were always afraid something like this might happen to you."

Chapter Two

I F I HADN'T BEEN so clueless, I might have seen it coming.

My first period that is. Not the tail. Never in a million years did I ever see *that* included in my life plan.

My period, though, should have been as plain as the zit on my face, which, no joke, took up half the real estate in that three-way mirror at Hyde's Department Store. Four hours earlier, that's where I'd stood, trying on bathing suits with the dressing room mirrors reflecting my gleaming white thighs into infinity.

Charming.

My muffin top of baby fat, peeking out from the two-piece tankini I was trying on, wasn't helping.

"Jade! Come out and show me." My best friend, Cori, called out from the other side of the dressing room door.

I pulled the tankini top down, trying to cover up my belly bulge. It sprang back with a snap.

"You're kidding, right?" There was no way I was letting

anyone see me in that thing. Who ever dreamed big girls could pull off midriff-baring, green sequins, anyway?

Why was I even doing this? I hated swimming.

"Come on, Jade. It can't be that bad." I could see Cori's tapping foot under the dressing room door. The drinking straw from her Slurpee squawked as she jammed it up and down through the cup's plastic cover.

"It's bad." I blew a curl from my forehead. This was bathing suit number eleven. Things were *not* going well. "You know, my dad has a conference in Dallas the day of your pool party. We could save ourselves a lot of trouble if I just went with him."

"Forget it. The perfect suit is out there." I was beginning to feel like a Cori Blake Fashion Project. "I won't give up until we find it."

"That's comforting."

Cori's straw went silent. Her open-toe slingbacks spun around and pointed out into the store.

"Jade…" she whispered through the door.

"What?"

"It's him."

"Who?" I tugged at the tankini some more. It was no use.

"Luke. You know, he's a year ahead of us? I thought he went on some sailboat cruise or something." Port Toulouse was known for its great sailing, but taking six months off school to sail the high seas was still big news.

"Luke *Martin?*" I muttered. "Can you hear my eyes rolling?"

The guy was so full of himself he could barely remember my name. Or, maybe he'd just blocked it from his memory after that unfortunate spin-the-bottle incident at Jenn McFadden's eleventh birthday party. How was I supposed to know I'd trip over the bottle? Or that a face-on collision with my braces would send him to the emergency room for stitches?

"Yeah, you should see his tan."

I tried to follow along as Cori went on about Luke's sun-bleached hair and cute surfer shorts, but the only thing occupying my mind at that moment was the fact that—even through all the miracles of modern science— they *still* hadn't invented a bathing suit that didn't creep up your butt. Maybe my brilliant engineer dad could get to work on *that* instead of trying to unify the theories of the universe.

"Here. Hold this." Cori handed me her Slurpee over the dressing room door. A few napkins fluttered to the floor.

"You're not leaving me here, are you?" I rubbed my temples to ease the pounding headache building up behind my right eyeball.

"Be right back."

I took a swig of the Slurpee but the sickeningly sweet sludge made me gag.

Ew. Ew. Ew.

Definitely not the effect I was going for. I plunked the cup on the bench along with the fallen napkins and yanked off the tankini, cursing the fact that I'd agreed to do this in the first place. But it was Cori's first pool party *ever* in a few weeks, which meant wearing a bathing suit, which meant a trip to Hyde's since I'd thrown out all my suits from the year before. Not like they would have fit anymore, anyway.

I heard a sound.

"Cori?"

Nope. Probably just the dressing room attendant picking up the merchandise from the stall next to mine. Guilt set in, so I started to hang bathing suits from the pile on the floor, but the straps kept slipping off the hangers. Between that and Cori holding me hostage until we found the perfect bathing suit (she hid my shoes), I was working on a full-on crank session.

So yeah, mood swings, zit, headache…oh, and cramps—did I mention cramps? The "first period" evidence was mounting; I just didn't know it yet.

What I *did* know was if I didn't get out of that dressing room *toot sweet*, I was sure to slip into a spandex-induced coma.

Finally, Cori's slingbacks reappeared.

"I can't believe you ditched me for that guy," I complained.

"Sorry, just had to get a closer look. Did you know he has a brother?"

"Older or younger?"

"Older. His name is Trey."

"Hopefully, a less obnoxious version of Luke. Can I have my shoes back?"

"Nice try."

"Come on, Cori." I closed my eyes and rested my head against the door. "I've already demolished the whole swim-wear section. There can't be much left out there."

"I didn't forget about you," Cori said. Clinking hangers sounded from the other side of the door. "Here, try this one. It's got three-way stretch and a shelf bra." Cori slapped a suit over the top of the dressing room door. The girl was incessant.

"It's got JIGGY written across the butt."

"That's the brand name," Cori said.

"You're kidding, right?"

"What? It's cute!" Cori insisted.

"On you, maybe. There's no way I'm stretching JIGGY across my behind." Another one for the pile.

"Okay, okay. Try this one." She whacked another suit over the door. "It's got a minimizer waist and shirring across the top to enhance your bust line." Cori was obvi-ously keeping up with the current season of *Real Runway* on the Zest Channel.

"It's another one of those tankinis." I dropped the suit to my side when I noticed the two pieces. Muffin top alert.

"Yeah, but I got it in a tall so the top should be long enough to cover your stomach. Try it on."

I couldn't even get mad at her for pointing out my "problem area." Cori might have been a total knockout but she didn't ever make me feel bad about how I looked. I knew she was just trying to help.

"Okay. But after this, I am done. I'll walk out of here barefoot if I have to." I pulled on the tankini bottoms over my granny panties (100% cotton and maximum butt coverage) then turned to check out my profile.

Okay. Not bad.

I reached for the top and pulled it off its hanger. Pretty good, so far. Deep coral blue with a filmy overlayer across the top. I was about to pull it on over my head when the tag stitched to the inside of the lining stopped me. The brand name was scrawled across the tag in white cursive writing.

Michaela.

My mother's name.

I stared at the letters, unable to tear my eyes away. It brought me instantly to that day at Gran's cottage in Dundee. The rowboat ride. Mom's smiling face, framed with long, ebony hair. The late afternoon swim. The sudden yell. The splashing. I blinked the sting of the memory away. A little cough-like, choking sound got caught in the back of my throat.

Don't cry. Don't cry.

"Have you been sucked into a portal in there or do you have that thing on yet?" Cori asked.

"Cori?"

"Yeah?"

"Look." I stuck my hand over the door and showed her the tag.

"Oh!" Cori and I had known each other ever since our

moms met at a Stroller Striders walking club back when we were in diapers. I practically lived at her house for months after Mom drowned. She understood right away. "You *have* to try it on now."

"I'm not sure…" I held the suit to my face, expecting the familiar scent of Mom's Peachtree Pro-vitamin shampoo or something. But of course, the suit gave no hints that it was anything but just that. A bathing suit.

But still.

"Just try it! I promise I'll give you back your shoes if it doesn't fit."

"Okay," I whispered. My hands trembled as I shrugged into the bathing suit top. The fabric slipped down along my upper body, the straps nestled perfectly into the curve of my shoulders. And best of all, the hem met the top of the tankini bottoms with an inch to spare.

"Wow."

"Let's see!" Cori yelled.

This time, I opened the door and stepped out. Cori's eyes grew wide as she looked me over.

"It's perfect." Her face broke into a huge smile.

"Yeah?" I turned to look at myself in the mirror again. The color, the style, the material: it was like someone had made it especially for me. And with my mom's name stitched on the tag, there was no way this wasn't The One. "Mom would have loved this," I murmured.

"Does this mean you'll come to my pool party?" Cori asked.

"The odds are improving." I turned from side to side, checking my reflection from each angle.

"Oh, yay! This is going to be so much fun!" Cori hugged me hard and we did that little jumpy, huggy thing we always did when we were excited. Who knew a bathing suit could bring on so much joy?

Only, that jumpy, huggy thing must have brought on something else because all of a sudden, I felt a gush of something warm and damp between my legs.

I stiffened.

"What?" Cori asked.

Ding, ding, ding!

"Nothing."

Actually—something.

My period. My first period. Right there, in the middle of Hyde's Department Store. I ducked back into the dressing room and slammed the door.

"I'm just so…"

Oh, no. Oh, no. Oh, no.

"…so happy!"

I pulled off the bathing suit bottoms. A darkened stain ran off the side of the hygienic strip. Then I checked my granny panties and yup—a bright, red spot.

Great. Just great.

"What are you doing in there?" Cori asked.

I should say something. But I couldn't. Not since the Lie.

We were twelve. Sleepover. Confession time. Cori had

just gotten her first period, and all the older girls had theirs already, so I kind of (just a teensy bit) let on that I'd had my period too. Yes, it was wrong. Yes, I felt like a big, fat loser. But I figured it was only a matter of time. How was I supposed to know I'd have to perpetuate the myth for almost *two more years?*

I poked my head out the dressing room door and tried to look normal.

"Just taking off the *best* bathing suit *ever* so we can finally get out of here." I forced a smile and shut the door. I yanked the stack of Super Sonic Slurpee napkins from under the cup and stuffed them in my underwear.

Cori's cell phone rang. I hurried to get dressed and hung up the tankini, fastening it with the hanger's large metal clips. Cori chatted for a couple of minutes, then snapped her phone shut.

"That was Lainey," Cori called through the door. "She's gonna meet us at the food court."

"Lainey?" I wasn't sure I was ready to fess up to Cori right then, but I *really* didn't want to spill my guts in front of Lainey Chamberlain.

What to do...what to do...

"I'm sorry," Cori said. "I forgot to tell you I called her to get my dress sketches back. Do you mind?" Lainey's mom was a fashion designer with her own studio and boutique. She had been reviewing Cori's portfolio.

"Oh, no, no. It's not that." I gathered up the Michaela bathing suit and stepped out of the dressing room, avoiding Cori's gaze. I needed to buy some time to figure out what to do. Time to decide how to tell Cori I'd been lying to her all this, um, time. "Why don't you go meet up with Lainey while I pay? I'll catch up with you guys once I'm done."

"No, it's okay. I'll wait," Cori said.

Not the right answer! I couldn't just walk around the mall with a Super Sonic Slurpee napkin wedgie. I needed to get myself to a washroom first to get order restored in my nether regions. Maybe I could get something from that big, white maxi pad–vending machine box thingie. Hopefully I had a quarter.

"Nah, I'm going to be a bit. I still have to find my dad to tell him where we'll be. Plus," I lowered my voice, "I don't know if it was that breakfast burrito I had this morning, but I *really* need to use the facilities."

Cori laughed and handed me my shoes. "Meet us at Paco's Tacos."

I arranged the tankini on the conveyor belt at the checkout, making sure the stain on the bottoms was well hidden by the top. Whatever the price, I couldn't leave that bathing suit behind. Especially since:

1. If I didn't buy it, it would raise all sorts of embarrassing questions from Cori.
2. You break it, you buy it. Darn moral fiber.
   And last, but not least:
3. My mom's name was stitched on the tag.

Those three things, combined, pretty much sealed the deal.

"Did you find everything you were looking for?" the cashier (or *Hello, my name is: Gladys*) asked.

I nodded and stared at the conveyor belt as it whirred forward. Gladys picked up the tankini and started pulling it off the hanger.

"I need that hanger!" I blurted.

"That's fine, honey." She continued to pull at the suit. "But all items must be removed from their hangers to scan them. Company policy."

The tankini bottoms fell in a heap on the conveyor belt. I grabbed for them.

"Is this a two-piece?" Gladys reached for the bottoms and looked at me funny when I wouldn't let go. I dropped my hand and smiled weakly. She donned her glasses, hanging from a gold chain around her neck, and turned the two pieces over and over, trying to find a tag.

She's going to see. She's going to see.

Gladys yelled over to the next checkout.

"Sylvia? Are we selling this as a two-piece?" She waved the top and bottom in each hand, high up in the air. I blinked away the sparkly dancing squiggles from my vision and tried not to puke.

Sylvia looked up from her register. "Call Swimwear."

"*Swimwear to checkout 3. Swimwear, checkout 3. Customer waiting.*" Gladys' voice rang over the intercom.

I wondered how long human beings could hold their

breath before passing out since I was sure I was bordering on three minutes already. I could imagine the Swimwear person coming over. They'd see the stain for sure. They might even bust me for the chaos I'd left in the dressing room. Security would escort me out to the parking lot and alert the media. I could imagine the headlines:

Freak-of-Nature, Jade Baxter, gets First Period Four Weeks from Fourteen.

Ruins stock at local Hyde's Department Store.

Full story at six.

"It's a tankini," Swimwear said when the lady finally arrived.

I must have sighed a bit too enthusiastically because Gladys gave me a bitter look. "It goes on our shift report if we punch it in wrong."

I dropped my gaze and fumbled in my bag for my wallet.

Gladys rang up the bathing suit and my whole body relaxed when she finally placed it in the bag. I paid, mumbled a thank you and stuffed the receipt in my wallet.

Finally! Free at last!

I slammed into a row of shopping carts as I rushed for the exit to the mall.

"Hey, not so fast!" Gladys yelled.

Pain shot through my hip as I turned to face her. Had she seen the stain? Did it finally occur to her what it was?

"Yes?" I whimpered.

Gladys looked at me over her jeweled half-glasses. She waved the hanger in the air. "I thought you said you wanted this."

"Oh, sorry! Thanks!" I doubled back to grab the hanger then charged for the exit to make my getaway.

Chapter Three

THE BATHROOM WAS A bust.

I had to wait for the cleaning lady to clear out and then my quarter got stuck in the maxi-pad machine, so I was left with no choice but to make the trek to Dooley's Drugstore a little farther down the mall.

Did I even know what to get once I got there?

I rushed past the food court, hoping Cori and Lainey didn't see me and tried not to waddle as I approached Dooley's, but the Super Sonic Slurpee napkin situation was making things a bit tricky. My heart rate ramped up to a whirr as I pushed through the drugstore's turnstile to enter. I blinked back the glare from the stark, fluorescent lights. A cold sweat rose from every pore of my skin, covering me in a damp slick.

Nerves. Just nerves.

I tried to channel one of Dr. Becker's visualization techniques. She had a cottage close to Gran's and I'd gone to see her for counseling after Mom drowned.

Breathe in, two, three, four. Out, two, three, four. Go to your happy place.

Except my "happy place" was just about anywhere but there at that precise moment.

Priority number one: just get what I needed and high-tail it back to the washroom. I scanned the aisle markers and tried not to gag as I brushed past the perfume counter.

Hair and Hair Products

First Aid

Pain and Cold Remedies

Then, hung over aisle six, in print that seemed to be twice the size of everything else, there it was.

Feminine Hygiene Products

"Ouch!"

A leftover Mother's Day display jabbed into my other hip, balancing out my shopping cart injury. At this rate, I'd need a walker before I even made it through puberty. A few greeting cards fluttered to the floor.

On this Mother's Day

The Meaning of Mommy

Yo, Momma!

I hurried to stash the cards back onto the display and tried to stay focused. Especially since my Slurpee napkin wedgie was beginning to slip.

I made it to aisle six, avoiding any more injuries, and walked partway down the row, glancing around to make sure Cori hadn't decided to restock on cherry blast lip gloss. A mother struggled by with a rubber band of a toddler, forcing me to plaster my body against the opposite shelf to let them through.

What I wouldn't give to have Mom there. But Mom was gone. Plus, Dad was probably sitting on a bench in the middle of the mall, Googling random facts on his Blackberry, and Cori was totally in the dark about what was going on thanks to the Lie.

I was on my own with this one.

Once the coast was clear, I turned to face the dizzying display of flower and butterfly packaging in varying shades of pinks, purples, and whites. This was nothing like the panty liner commercials with the girl in the flowing dress, prancing through fields of daisies. How was I supposed to choose from the millions upon millions of choices spread over a ten-acre radius of super absorbency?

White plastic tags hung from the shelves.

Super Maxi $6.25
Easy Glide $4.49
Sheerlights $7.99

Gah! Money!

I tucked my Hyde's Department Store bag under my arm and rifled through my purse for funds. Half eaten cookie, a dead Tic Tac, the can of pepper spray Dad insisted I carry when I walked home by myself that week when Cori had the measles.

"Aim for the eyes and look away," Dad had coached. I couldn't imagine any shady characters in Port Toulouse I'd ever have to pepper spray, but whatever.

I frowned at the pathetic amount of money I had left. Just as I'd expected.

The tankini had set me back quite a bit, so all I had left was a grand total of four bucks (I fished in my pocket) and twenty-seven cents.

What was I supposed to do now?

"Jade! How'd you make out?"

I jumped so high, I'm sure I caught air. Another headline flashed through my mind:

Caught on Pharmacy Surveillance Tape:

Plus-sized teenaged girl jumps three feet, clean out of her skin.

More at 11.

"Dad! What are you doing here?" I clutched the money to my chest. How did he know where to find me? Was I emanating some kind of first period hormone? I watched the Nature Channel—these things could happen.

Dad smiled. "I needed shaving cream and spotted you on my way to the checkout."

"Oh."

"Did you find what you were looking for?"

"Wha…?" I blinked.

Dad's gaze shifted to the Hyde's bag, now in a heap beside me on the floor. "Looks like a successful shopping trip."

The bathing suit. Of course.

"Oh, yeah!" I held up the bag and shifted uncomfortably as the Slurpee napkins nagged at my girly bits. "Success!"

"So, are you ready to go? Where's Cori?" Dad looked past me.

"Uh, she met up with a friend at the food court. I just

had to make a little pit stop." Then I stopped myself. "To find you, that is. How *are* you, anyway?" I wrapped my arm around Dad's shoulder and tried to steer him down the aisle.

"So you thought you'd look for me in the…" Dad twisted his head around to get a look at where we were. "…tampon aisle?"

I stopped. What was I doing? I couldn't leave the store without buying something to replace the wad of napkins in my underwear, and since I was short on cash, I had no choice but to cave.

"Um, Dad?" The words got stuck in the back of my throat like a gob of sticky peanut butter.

"Yes?"

"Well," I stammered. "See, it's like this." How was I gonna approach this? I decided to get straight to the point and admit to another, um, misrepresentation of the truth. "Yeah, remember a couple of months ago when you were on the phone with work and I asked you for ten bucks to go to the drug store?"

Accessing. Accessing. I could see the data being analyzed behind his eyes like the little egg timer doodad on the computer when it's loading files.

"Oh!"

Bingo.

"You mean for…" He glanced around the aisle.

Well that's what he'd *assumed* anyway. I know. It looked bad. First Cori, now this. But, to my credit, I didn't exactly *lie* to him, though it was time to set things straight.

"Yeah, only, I didn't actually have my period then."

"You didn't?" Dad's face contorted in confusion. Why he hadn't noticed that the girly stuff never made it to the bathroom closet was beyond me, but I cut him some slack on that one.

"Not until today, that is." I raised an eyebrow in a hopeless arc.

Dad seemed to be calculating the density of air as he sorted this out in his mind. Then finally, his face came to attention.

"Ah, so you mean?" He scanned the shelves. Then his eyes came back to meet mine. "And you?"

I nodded.

Dad put a hand on my shoulder and looked at me for a long moment. His mouth softened into a smile. "Don't worry," he gave me a quick wink, "I'll get a basket."

I sighed, relieved to have another person on the planet who understood what I was going through.

"Thanks, Dad."

Maybe Mom wasn't there, but it was all going to be okay.

If there was one thing I knew, it was that I could always count on Dad.

When Dad said "basket," I pictured one of those handheld, plastic jobbies with the metal handles. But when he rounded the corner of aisle six with a full-sized shopping cart, I seriously considered running and screaming for the food court and confessing everything to Cori.

She'd forgive me for lying, wouldn't she? She'd come tell me what I needed to buy.

Anything but this.

Dad studied the screen of his Blackberry and pushed the cart toward me with his free hand. "Medzine Online says that the typical volume of blood loss per menstrual period ranges from 10 to 35 milliliters."

"Are you *Googling* this?"

"Menorrhagia could see flows in excess of 80 milliliters." Dad tapped his index finger to his lips and scanned the shelves.

"Men-a-what?" Could this be any more humiliating?

But Dad didn't hear me. He was too busy price checking and comparison shopping. My overflowing pool of confidence in Dad was quickly being drained.

"Let's just grab something and go." I reached for a package of extra-long something-or-others and was about to throw them in the basket, I mean, cart.

"Just a sec." Dad held up a hand, his gaze never leaving the screen of his BlackBerry. "Better get two of those." Then he picked up a blue and yellow box from the shelf. "What are these Easy Glide things?"

"Read…the…package," I said between clenched teeth. The Slurpee napkins were now working themselves around the edge of my underwear and threatened to slip down my right pant leg. I was in no mood to negotiate with the Tampon Terrorist.

"Oh! Jade." Dad looked up from his BlackBerry and

eyed me seriously. "Are you experiencing cramping, loose bowel movements, and acne? Maybe we should get something for that too."

"Dad!"

"What?" Dad asked, dropping his hand to his side.

"I'll see you at the check-out," I muttered.

I turned to go, leaving Dad to his research. Maybe I could just swipe another wad of Slurpee napkins and call it a day. Or better yet, those nice, big Paco's Tacos ones might provide better coverage. All this was running through my mind as I stormed away, skirted by claims of super absorbency and dry weave. At the end of the aisle though, I ran into something tall, dark and...

"Luke!"

My Hyde's bag fell to the floor as we collided. Luke's bag fell too. I bent to pick mine up, only to bonk heads with him as he tried to do the same.

"Oh! Sorry." An uncontrollable chuckle escaped from my throat. Yeah, real smooth, Jade. Injure the poor guy, then laugh at him. It was like spin-the-bottle all over again.

Luke straightened, rubbed his head, and smiled, no doubt stunned by the blow. He handed me my bag.

"Um...Jayden, right?" He turned his head a bit to the side and squinted.

So, he *did* remember me. Well, kind of. At least it was better than the "Scissor Lips" nickname he'd given me in fifth grade.

"Yes. Well. It's Jade, actually." I took my bag from him

and nodded slowly, trying not to be too obvious while I checked him out. Okay, so maybe I was still a *bit* bitter, but I wasn't *blind*. Actually, it was the first time I'd been close enough to see the silvery scar my braces had inflicted above his right eyebrow. If I hadn't known better, the scar might have been considered rugged and mysterious.

And his sun-bleached curls *did* fall over his eyes in a pretty adorable way. Plus, Cori was right—killer tan.

But evil, I had to remind myself.

"Oh, right—Jade." Luke nodded. "Sorry about that."

Was Luke Martin actually apologizing? To me?

"That's okay. I get that a lot."

I did *NOT* get that a lot. Why was I making excuses for the guy? And why did I keep nodding and staring, with a ridiculous smile plastered across my face?

"You just look different without your braces," Luke said.

Aha! That braces comment was a dig. Definitely a dig. Well, whatever. I figured that would be it anyway. Pleasantly plump girl bumps into a cute (but evil) boy. A few polite words are exchanged. Girl and boy from parallel universes part ways, never to speak again. Isn't that how things should go?

But Luke just kept standing there, looking at me with the strangest expression. Did Luke actually want to keep talking to me?

"Um, Jade?"

"Yes?" I asked, expectantly.

He nodded to the bag I was holding in my other hand.

I looked down and wished I had a moron stick to beat myself senseless with, since all the time I was grinning like the village idiot, I'd had a death grip on his Dooley's Drugs bag.

"Oh!" I said, handing it to him. "Sorry."

"That's okay," Luke said with a grin.

"That. Bag. Yours." I pointed dumbly.

Sheesh. Such a firm grasp on the English language. But that only made Luke smile wider. Was he mocking me? Sure he was cute, but how did I know he wouldn't turn this into an opportunity to nail me with another nickname that would follow me through my high school years?

Okay. I had to salvage this conversation. There was no way I was leaving without at least one coherent sentence.

"Um, so you've been away, right?" I asked, real smooth-like. "Cruise boating or something? I mean sail shipping?"

Sail shipping? Ugh. *Much* better. Where was the moron stick when you really needed it?

"You mean sailing?" Luke was laughing now. "Yeah, we took a few months off to 'enrich our bonds as a family.'" He faked a serious tone but his eyes crinkled in the corners.

It was my turn to laugh.

"Oh, sorry." I stifled a snort. "Did your parents actually use that on you?"

"Yep. It was actually pretty cool though. It feels a bit weird to be back." Luke's expression seemed to change and I thought he might turn and leave any second.

"So, are you back in school now?" I asked, filling in

the dead air. Despite the shaky state of my underwear, I wanted to leave on a high note. Plus, there was just something…different about Luke since the last time I saw him.

"We're back for final exams," Luke said. "Mom home-schooled us while we were away, but she wanted to make sure she did a good job, I guess." He smiled. His perfect, straight, white teeth shone against his tanned skin.

"Teeth," I said vaguely. "I mean neat!" I waved my hand in the air to swat the word away.

Luke looked at me with an amused expression. He bunched up his bag in his hand and nodded his head.

"Well, see you around?"

Huh. That was nice. Not "Later, loser" or "Thanks for scarring me for life."

"Yeah, sure, Luke. See you around."

That was perfect. I'd finally managed to talk to Luke Martin without feeling like a complete idiot.

Luke was about to turn to go when we heard a commotion from down the aisle. We both looked up to see that Dad had managed to stock the shopping cart with every imaginable feminine hygiene product known to man. Um. Woman.

"Hey, Jade?" He called out holding two packages of maxi pads.

I shook my head violently to stop Dad from talking, but from where he stood, I doubted he could see I was talking to a boy. A mildly annoying, but nonetheless cute boy.

"Do you want wings or no wings?"

It was official.

This was shaping up to be the Most. Embarrassing. Day. Ever.

Chapter Four

I STARED OUT THE WINDOW, holding my throbbing head, as Dad wound the car along the main part of town, past the bank and thrift store. A few people window-shopped along Main Street, some pushing their way through the glass doors of Bridget's Diner, trying to beat the dinner rush. Though, "rush" was a bit of a stretch for our laid-back, oceanside town.

Dad drummed his thumbs on the steering wheel to the beat of the country music whining on the local radio station. We'd dropped Cori off a few minutes before, after the madness of the mall, and now Dad was trying to sell me on ordering Chef Chan for dinner but my whole body ached and my headache had been upgraded to a migraine thanks to a really annoying ring now developing in my ears.

"Sorry, Dad. I'm just not that into kung pao chicken tonight," I called over the music. "I just want to get home and crash."

The universe must have been conspiring against me because before we could cross the drawbridge at the canal, we caught a red light and a metal barrier swung down to block our way. A cabin cruiser sat in the boat lock below the bridge, waiting to sail through to Talisman Lake after making its way up the canal from the ocean. Warning bells clanged and the bridge drew open. I winced at the sound.

"Just great." I rested my forehead against the cool glass of the passenger-side window, wishing the day would just hurry up and be over.

"Might as well get comfortable." Dad put the car in park and rolled down his window to call out to Shaky Eddie in the boat lock's control tower. "Hiya, Eddie! Busy this week, eh?"

Eddie nodded and waved while he puffed on his cigarette, then he turned his attention back to the controls. Port Toulouse was famous for its mile-long water canal built between the ocean and the lake. It was Eddie's job to lead boats up the canal and into the boat lock, which acted like a holding tank. Depending on the tides, Eddie usually had to adjust the water level inside the lock to compensate for the difference between the ocean and the lake levels before boats could sail onward.

He'd let the Martins' sailboat through just a few days before, no doubt. I smiled, imagining the homecoming Eddie had given his grandsons, Luke and Trey, after so many months away.

The thought turned sour as I considered the impression I must have left on Luke at Dooley's. The guy probably thought I was a bigger dork than ever. But why the heck should it matter what he thought? At least he got his stitches out after a week. I was the one who was stuck with the "Scissor Lips" handle all through junior high.

"Well, have a good one!" Dad called out, rolling up his window. He turned to me, smiling, but must have sensed my desperation because he lowered the volume on the radio.

"Thank you," I muttered and rested my feet on the dashboard, trying to get comfy while we waited for the boat to pass through the lock.

"No problem, kiddo." Dad smiled. "Hey, how about we get some fries and 'wings' from Bridget's." He finger-quoted the wings part and winked. I know he was just trying to make up for the Dooley's episode, so I played along.

"You know, Dad? Geek humor is really tough to pull off."

"Thank you."

"That wasn't an endorsement." I rubbed my temples.

"Aw, come on, Jade." He gave my knee a little slap. "Where do you think you get your biting wit?"

"Well, if I'm supposed to get my sense of humor from you, what did I inherit from Mom?"

Mom. Maybe it was because my nerve endings were so raw, but for some reason she kept coming up over and over that day.

"Thank goodness you're more like her than me," he said quietly. "And the older you get, the more of her I see in you."

I glanced down and rubbed a chocolate stain from the

front of my shirt. "Yeah, right. Mom was tall and gorgeous. I don't look anything like her."

"Well..." Dad seemed to consider what to say next. "You'd be surprised how alike you both are. Take your feet, for instance. Here, show me your foot." He reached out his hand.

"No way!" I backhanded his arm.

"Come on. You'll see what I mean."

I eyed him and slid off one of my shoes.

Dad raised an eyebrow when he spotted the silver band around my pinkie toe. "What's this?"

"Um...a toe ring?" It's not like it was some big secret or anything.

"I guess I should be thankful it's not impaling your belly button."

"Don't worry; belly rings aren't really my thing. I prefer tattoos," I joked.

Dad ignored me and took my foot into his hand. I yanked it back. I'm beyond ticklish.

"I'm not trying to tickle you. I just want to show you something." He pulled my third and fourth toe apart. "See how these toes are webbed part way up? That's just like Michaela."

I pulled my shoe back on and muttered. "Great. I could have inherited Mom's flawless complexion, but instead, I got her weird feet."

Dad's forehead furrowed. "I always loved that about your mom."

A familiar blur gathered up in the corners of my eyes.

"Sorry, it's not that." I pulled my knees to my chest and let the tears I'd forced back earlier come streaming out.

"Ah, come here." Dad pulled me into a hug and rested his chin on top of my head.

I thought of the Michaela bathing suit and the fact that I just got my first period and the Mother's Day cards on the floor of the drugstore. Dad was doing his best, but shouldn't it be Mom there, getting me through this?

"It's just, well, for some reason, I really miss her today." My voice hiccupped the words into his shirt.

"I really miss her too," Dad rubbed my shoulder. "Weird feet and all."

Finally, the bells stopped clanging as the bridge lowered back into place. The barrier lifted to let us through. I stared at the cabin cruiser, now well on its way down the lake, as the car's tires thundered across the bridge's metal grating. After a few more minutes, we arrived home. I trudged up the walkway and dumped my stuff in the front hall once we got inside.

"I almost forgot." Dad fished something from the Dooley's bag while I kicked off my shoes. "I also got you some Epsom salt."

"What for?"

"Well..." He looked at me sheepishly. "A couple of Google links said that it's good for PMS symptoms since the magnesium sulfate draws toxins from the body, relaxes muscles, and sedates the nervous system."

I went to my happy place during that last bit of Dad's explanation. Still, a bath sounded like a good idea. I imagined soaking in the big claw foot tub upstairs. It would be a relief to get out of those yucky clothes and yucky underwear, and put the yucky day behind me.

"Okay," I said. "That's actually the best idea I've heard all day."

"Here." Dad put the Epsom salt back and passed the stuffed Dooley's bag to me. His face was kind and sweet. "Sorry I went a bit overboard at the drugstore, but I swear, it feels like I was taking the training wheels off your bike just last week. This is kind of uncharted territory for me."

"Me too," I whispered. I gave him a quick peck on the cheek and headed upstairs.

I locked the bathroom door behind me, tossed the Dooley's bag on the counter and turned on the water in the bath. The Epsom salt fizzed as the crystals met the stream of water. I found a spot for the leftover salt in the bathroom's linen closet. A plastic bottle toppled over at the back of the shelf. I pulled it out.

Peachtree Pro-vitamin. Mom's old shampoo.

The scent overwhelmed me when I clicked open the lid. I drank in the smell and closed my eyes. It was almost like Mom was there, holding me in a hug, her long hair in my face. Could she see me, wherever she was? Did she know how I was feeling, what I was thinking, just then? Did she know how much I missed her?

The sound of the flowing water pulled me from my thoughts. I snapped the lid shut and placed the bottle back on the shelf.

I stripped down to my underwear then wiped the steam from the bathroom mirror and took inventory.

Boobs? If I squished my arms together, I could almost convince myself I had cleavage.

Armpit check? Time to shave.

Other than that though, the same copper curls, squinty green eyes, and chubby cheeks met my gaze in the mirror. Same old Jade. Shouldn't I look different? Feel different? I was becoming a "woman" after all, wasn't I?

It took a while to fill the massive, old-fashioned tub, but I waited until it was a deep steaming pool before squeaking the tap closed. Then, it occurred to me. What would happen when I lowered myself into the water? Should I take a shower instead?

Think. Think.

I knew they'd covered this in Health Ed when they crammed all the girls into the school library and showed us those hideously embarrassing movies while the boys went outside to play flag football. But that was four years before and while 99% of those girls were sure to have gone through this already, I was left to wonder. It's not like I could just call up Cori (I still hadn't fessed up to the Lie) and I really didn't want Dad to fire up the search engine on this one.

I shrugged out of my underwear and eased myself into

the tub. The water wrapped its warmth around me, giving my whole body a feeling of weightlessness.

I waited.

Nothing.

I rested my head against the back of the tub, relieved and left feeling just a teensy bit stupid. But how was I supposed to know what would happen? Who tells you these things?

Then the harsh reality hit me.

Moms tell you these things.

In that moment, soaking in my Epsom salt bath, I missed Mom more than ever. A girl only gets her first period once in her life and I hated not knowing what to expect. I hated not knowing what to do.

And most of all, even though a wave of shame ran through me for letting the thought even enter my mind, I hated Mom for not being there and for leaving me to figure it all out.

I couldn't remember the exact moment I dozed off, but after crying until my eyes stung, the warm bath lulled me into one long, sleepy head nod.

I dreamt I was floating in the ocean, looking up at a cloudless sky, surrounded by long, white strands of silk. Purple and white jellyfish swayed in the current around me. But instead of being afraid of getting stung, their waving tentacles soothed me into a dreamy haze.

Was this my version of those goofy panty liner

commercials? I remembered thinking. No, this was different. It was peaceful and warm with no fields of daisies in sight.

My thoughts floated, suspended around me but close enough to touch. The silk danced in the water in curls, brushing up against my skin. I let the strips of fabric wrap around and around my arms and legs until I was enveloped in a cocoon of warmth.

I tried to remember a time when I'd felt so peaceful with the clear blue sky above and the motion of the waves all around but the bits of each thought were just beyond my reach. I closed my eyes and gave in to the soothing hum of the moment.

Then, something tugged the cloth from below.

The silk unwound from around me, sending me into a dizzying spin. I managed to free my arms and flailed in the water, but something kept pulling at the cloth, forcing me underwater. Water pushed its way down into my lungs. My legs stayed bound tightly and in my dreamlike state, I remembered thinking, if only I could free them, I might stand a chance of saving myself before being dragged to the bottom of the ocean...

A knocking sound broke the spell.

"Jade?" Dad's voice worked through my dream. "You okay, honey?"

I awoke, coughing and thrashing in the water around me, still confused by the images swirling in my mind.

The cloth, the sky, the ocean.

The bathroom, cold water—I was in the tub.

Rubbing my eyes, blinking away the sting, trying to get out, shocked by what I saw breaking through the surface of the water.

Then, I was yelling for Dad, he was crashing through the door.

And I had a tail. A shimmering, scale-covered, slimy, wet tail.

Freak-of-nature suddenly took on a whole new meaning.

Chapter Five

THE ONLY THING MORE unbelievable than the fact that my lower body now looked like a yellow-finned tuna was the idea that Dad might actually know something about it. I hammered him with questions as he drained the water from the tub.

"What the heck do you mean, you were always afraid something like this might happen to me? What do you know about this?"

Dad made a few attempts at words as he draped a towel around me and lifted me from the bathtub. Not an easy task since I was now slipperier than a wriggly trout.

This couldn't be real, could it? No. It was a joke. It had to be.

"Oh, I get it!" I laughed out loud. "This is for that ten bucks I wheedled out of you when you were on the phone with work, isn't it? Ha-ha, good one, Dad. How'd you get this thing on without waking me up?" I pushed at the tail, trying to see where it connected but the transition from skin to scales was seamless.

"This isn't a joke," Dad said in a low voice as he sat me down on my bed.

I squeezed my eyes shut to try to keep the room from spinning. Of course it wasn't a joke. Dad had been locked on the other side of the bathroom door when it happened. Still, I couldn't get myself to believe any of it.

"Are you telling me this thing is actually *attached* to my body?!" I gasped. The reality of what was happening made my stomach lurch. Dad must have noticed because he shoved the wastepaper basket in front of me just in time for me to toss my cookies.

"Oh, Jade. Are you okay?" Dad fussed over me. He tucked my hair behind my ear and handed me tissues to wipe my mouth.

I collapsed against the pillows again and tried to catch my breath. "No. I am not okay. This is NOT okay!"

"Let's just get you comfortable…" Like what a nurse would say to some poor patient in a hospital ward. This was wrong. Seriously wrong.

"I don't need to get comfortable! I need to get this thing off!" I shook the tail through the air, but it stayed stuck. I was crying by then—crazy, wailing, wounded harp seal kind of cries.

"Shh, shh…I'm so sorry, Jade. I'm just not sure how to explain this." Dad draped a sweater around my shaking frame and covered the tail with a blanket.

"Try me!" I searched his tortured face. He sat in the chair next to my bed and ran his hand through his hair. Typical Dad stress signal.

"There is something I haven't told you because I wasn't sure I'd ever have to." He rested his elbows on his knees, lacing and unlacing his fingers. "Your mom and I…"

"What about Mom?" The sound of her name had me bracing my hands against the mattress.

Dad squeezed his eyes shut. "Just let me gather my thoughts, will you, Jade? This isn't an easy thing to explain."

"And you think being covered in fish scales is *easy?*" My face screwed up in an involuntary sob.

"Oh, sweetie."

"I'm sorry." I wiped my nose with the sleeve of the sweater. "I'm just…" I struggled to catch my breath "…a little freaked out here."

That was the understatement of the year.

"No, no. Don't be sorry." Dad stood and paced the room, letting out a huge, noisy breath. "Don't ever be sorry about this." He waved his hand toward the lump under the blanket where my legs used to be.

"What exactly *is* this?" I slapped the blanket, sending a sting through my thigh. Ah! Not my thigh. Not anymore!

Dad cleared his throat. "Your mom and I always planned on telling you. But after she…" He drew in a breath and blinked a few times before continuing. "After Michaela drowned, I wondered if the secret would die along with her."

"What secret?" I fought to keep the edge out of my voice, but the scales on the tail began to prickle. A lot. Was searing scale pain normal? I wondered. Then again, could anything about having a tail be considered *normal?*

Dad sat and took my hand in his. "Jade…"

"Yes?"

He took a deep breath. "Michaela…your mom…she was a mermaid."

I looked at him for a full ten seconds before my brain caught up with his words.

"A…a wha?"

"A Pesco-sapien. Part fish, part aquatic humanoid."

Of all the times to pull the science card on me. I closed my eyes and shook my head in disbelief.

"I know what a mermaid is! But Mom was a person. A human. She walked upright. She had legs! What the heck do you mean—a mermaid?" None of it came even close to registering. That afternoon, my biggest problem had been trying to find a bathing suit that fit and getting my first period. Now, the complexity of my life seemed to get jacked up by a few hundred decimal points.

"Well, technically I guess I should say she *used* to be a mermaid." He squeezed my hand. "Ah, Jade, I know none of this makes sense. I didn't understand it either, when I first met Micci."

"Then I'm…" I couldn't quite finish the sentence before being sent down another spiral of disbelief.

"It seems so." Dad let out a desperate sigh and leaned heavily against the back of the chair.

"But how is that even possible?" Then I looked at him seriously. "Please tell me Mom was human when you met her." I had enough to try to wrap my head around without imagining the obvious.

Dad let out a little laugh.

"We met about a year after she was washed ashore during Hurricane Jade."

"I was named after a hurricane?" I could believe almost anything now.

He nodded. "From what Micci told me, she was knocked unconscious and washed ashore during the storm. By the time she made it back to the ocean, she'd pulmo-morphed."

I closed my eyes and shook my head.

"Speak English!" I shifted in the bed, trying to get comfortable, but the scales went from prickling to burning and my whole lower body was a furnace of heat.

"Her gills and lungs had changed too much from breathing air. It made it harder for her to survive underwater."

I brought my hands to my face and shook my head. "This is unbelievable."

"There was this group of mer-people called the Mermish Council, I think, who had just taken over the government," Dad continued. "They were really cracking down on mer-security and they worried your mom may lose consciousness some day, since her underwater breathing had become so compromised. They couldn't risk her getting washed up on shore again and being discovered, so they allowed her to become human."

"They kicked her out of the ocean?" Thoughts swam

around in my head, like the white flecks in a just-shaken snow globe.

"I'm a bit unclear on the details." Dad took off his glasses. He began to clean them with a handkerchief from his pocket and shook his head as he rubbed. "Your mom didn't like to talk about it much; I suspect it may have been some sort of Mermish Code of Silence. What I *do* know is that the transformation from mermaid to human was very long and difficult for her."

"But how can a human…and a mermaid even…?"

He put his glasses back on. "There was obviously a stray branch on the evolutionary tree."

"But I can't live like this! What about school? My friends?"

"I'm not sure."

"Then we have to find this Mermish Committee or Council or whatever and fix this! We can fix this, can't we?"

Dad stood and stared out the window. That's when I realized, he didn't know that either.

The heat from the tail wafted up from beneath the blankets and filled the air around me, making it hard to breathe. Or maybe my lungs had changed when I slipped underwater in the bathtub, just like Mom's had when she got washed ashore. Did I now have gills I didn't know about?

"Something's wrong." I pulled back the blankets to let the heat escape. The scales on the tail glowed like the orangey-red shade of a blazing sunset.

"What is it?" Dad turned and read my tortured expression. He ran to my side.

"Ah!" A rush of adrenaline shot through my body, putting all of my cells on red alert. Searing pain pierced through the tail as one by one, the scales shifted and morphed into a shiny film.

"It looks like the scales are turning back into skin," Dad whispered.

"It hurts!" I pulled myself up on my elbows. As each scale morphed into skin, it left a stab of pain in its place. I gasped for breath, as the throbbing took over. A crease deepened along the length of the tail.

"What can I do? Jade, just tell me…"

"Make it stop!" I looked up into Dad's face, tears blurring my eyes.

"I'm not sure what to do…" Dad's face crumpled as he arranged and rearranged the pillows around me. Finally, he gave up and pulled me into his arms. "Just breathe, honey, breathe."

My whole body wracked with pain as the tip of the tail split. I collapsed against Dad's chest but couldn't tear my eyes away from what was happening. The separation made its way up the deepening crease, dividing the tail in two. The scales had merged into a solid surface and now shone pink like the color of sunburned skin.

"I think you're changing back!" Dad rocked me back and forth and stroked my hair. But nothing could distract me from the unbelievable agony.

"Look!" Horror and relief swept over me as the tips of the tail fin curled onto themselves and divided into ten bits, reforming my toes. Jolts of energy spread through the two divided sections of the tail, shaping my feet, my knees, my thighs, and finally, my hips and torso.

"It's okay, honey. Breathe," Dad whispered into my hair.

I gave in to the agony and moaned as the last bits of my former mermaid self dissolved into my skin. In moments, the change was complete.

I fell back against my pillows, exhausted. Goose bumps rose along my damp skin.

"You're human again," Dad whispered. He pulled the wet towels and blankets onto the floor and draped Gran's afghan over me.

"How?" I tried to pull the clues of what just happened together, but nothing made sense. "Why now? Why today?"

"Maybe…" Dad paused "…I don't know."

For once in his life, he didn't seem to have an answer. No amount of science or reason could explain what had just happened.

"What if it happens again?" The tears returned. One part relief, one part fear, one part wishing Mom were there to help me understand what had just happened. I needed to keep talking, to try to make sense of it all.

"Shh, shh." Dad stroked my hair. We sat there for a long moment. He kept his arm around me as I gave myself over to the numbing exhaustion. Soon, my eyes grew heavy and my breathing deepened.

"Why don't you get into your pajamas and get some

sleep?" he suggested. "We can talk more about this in the morning. I promise."

I popped awake and wiped the drool from the side of my mouth. Nice.

"Okay-um." I slurred the word. Then I remembered. I'd have to go sort things out in the bathroom before collapsing.

"I just need to make a pit stop," I said mechanically. It seemed strange to be thinking so practically after what had just happened but at that point my mind and body went into autopilot.

I swung my legs (my legs!) over to the side of the bed and braced a hand on the headboard to stand. My whole body shook as my feet met the floor, filling me with worry. Could I actually walk?

"Do you need help?" Dad asked.

"Yes," I whispered, barely finding my voice. I leaned heavily against him, my legs still stinging from the transformation.

Dad draped the afghan over my shoulders and helped me as I hobbled to the bathroom. "Thank goodness you're back to normal." His voice was heavy with relief.

I managed a smile before shutting the door of the bathroom.

Normal. I braced my hands against the vanity and stared at my reflection in the mirror.

I had a feeling there was no way I would ever feel normal again.

Chapter Six

...4 days Post-Tail

I NEARLY FELL OUT OF bed when a high-pitched ring pierced through my dream. I fumbled through the bedside table and whacked the snooze button on my alarm clock.

No relief.

What was that noise? That horrible noise? Demons from the underworld? Tortured feral cats? Wild, screaming banshees?

My hand finally found the phone. Without thinking, I pressed TALK.

"Hellumph?" I mumbled and rubbed my eyes.

"Jade! Are you okay? I've been trying to call you for days. Did your dad give you my messages?"

I sat up in bed and was instantly awake.

"Cori! Oh, um, yeah. Sorry. Been a bit sick. Why are you calling so early on a Saturday?" I wriggled my toes under the covers, relieved that the change from mermaid to girl had stuck for one more day.

"It's after one."

I turned to the window. The sun filtered through the blinds, cascading rippled lines of light across my blankets. I rubbed the sleep from my eyes and looked at the clock.

One fifteen.

"Are you feeling any better?" Cori continued.

"Um. Yeah. I guess."

"Rough week?" she asked.

"You could say that again." I fell back into my pillows and cradled the phone to my ear.

"Sounds like more than just the flu. What's up?" she asked.

"Oh, just stuff." I paused and considered what to say. I hadn't exactly been in the right headspace to tell Cori the truth about my period since the mall, but that was nothing compared to everything else weighing on my mind.

But where to begin? The beginning seemed like a good place.

"I guess seeing my mom's name in that bathing suit the other day kind of weirded me out."

"Yeah, I can imagine. But it looks really amazing on you."

A strange chill crept along my skin.

"You think?" I brought the comforter around my neck to warm myself.

"Trust me," Cori said.

I sighed. "Thanks, Cori. But there's something else…"

"What?"

"Well…" I stammered. I had to at least admit to the Lie. That would be a start. "I know you think I got my period a couple of years ago, but…"

"But what?"

"Well, you know when I came out with the bathing suit on and we hugged and stuff? That's actually when it happened."

"Your first period? You mean..."

"Yeah, and I didn't know how to tell you 'cause I'd been kinda lying to you all this time."

Cori didn't answer. I pressed on. There was no turning back now.

"So I had to stuff a wad of Super Sonic Slurpee napkins in my underwear until I got to Dooley's."

I could hear a muffled sound on the other end of the line. Was she upset? Oh, great! Did I make her *cry?*

"Are you okay?" I asked.

"I'm sorry..." Cori laughed out loud. "Super... Slurpee..." She sputtered out the words.

I smiled with relief.

"Yeah, and then my dad packed the shopping cart full of about a zillion different kinds of maxi pads and tampons..."

By then, we were both trying to talk between fits of giggles.

"You...you had to go to the drugstore with your Dad?" More laughing. "That's...the funniest thing...ever."

We finally caught our breath. It was time for me to apologize.

"I'm happy to be a source of amusement but I'm really sorry I lied."

"You dope," Cori said. "You know you can tell me any-thing, right?"

"I know." But could I?

"So let that trip to Dooley's with your dad be a lesson to you: no more secrets. From now on, full disclosure, okay?"

"Okay," I said quietly, considering the other very big secret I had to tell. But I couldn't tell Cori I was part mermaid just then. Not like that. Not on the phone.

Cori continued. "Oh, I just got a text from Lainey. She wants to grab a burger at Bridget's. You feeling up to it?"

"Lainey, huh?" Not that I had anything against Lainey Chamberlain, but ever since Cori bonded with her over pashminas at Lainey's mom's boutique, it seemed like our duo was quickly becoming a trio. Besides, I kinda wanted Cori to myself that day. We still had a lot more to talk about.

"Yeah, and guess what?" Cori continued. "Mrs. Chamberlain liked a few of my dress designs and said I might be able to do my co-op mentorship with her next year!"

"That's amazing!" I could imagine the smile on Cori's face. "But promise me that when you get to be a big famous clothing designer, you'll never design anything with green metallic sequins."

She laughed. "Don't worry. I think we can both agree that green metallic sequins are a crime against humanity."

"And never, ever appliqué the word JIGGY on anyone's butt."

We were laughing hysterically again.

"So, are you gonna come? There's a Bridget Burger with your name on it," Cori said.

"Mm…Bridget Burger…tempting."

"And waffle fries," she reminded me.

Then I remembered my leg status. Sure, nothing had happened since Tuesday night but I'd stayed in the house since then. What if I merma-cized again in the middle of Bridget's Diner?

"You know?" My voice turned shaky. "I'm just getting up and I'm not sure how I feel yet. If you don't see me at Bridget's in an hour, just go ahead and order without me."

"All right," Cori paused, "but are you sure you're okay? You still sound a bit strung out."

Strung out pretty much covered it.

"Um, no, I'm fine. Really." I faked a laugh.

"Okay…if you're sure," Cori said.

But I wasn't sure. Lying about my period was one thing, but now I was keeping another secret, an even *bigger* secret from her. But later. I'd tell her later when we were alone. Actually, it would be good to have Cori to talk to.

"Well, there is something else, but we can talk about it when I see you, okay?"

"Sure," Cori said slowly, "but call me if you can't make it. I'll get you some waffle fries to go."

"You rock. Thanks, Cori."

We said our good-byes and I hung up the phone. Cori really was the best friend ever. I smiled and thought of all the times she had listened to me talk about Mom that past year. She'd been amazing through it all. Yeah, she'd freak when I told her what had happened, but Cori was like a sister to me. It would feel good to be totally honest with her again.

No secrets. Full disclosure.

"Hey, Jade. You feeling okay?" The door squeaked as Dad opened it a crack.

"Mmm-hmm, yeah, I think so. You can come in." I scraped my mess of curls into a hair tie from my bedside table.

Dad entered, carrying a laundry basket. He set it down on my dresser.

"I checked on you a little earlier, but you were still comatose. Did you have a good sleep?"

"Yeah, thanks." I smiled then noticed the shadow of stubble lining Dad's jaw. His hair poked out at all angles. "You, on the other hand, look like you've seen better days. Although, if you're going for the aging, burnt-out rocker look, you've totally nailed it."

"Insolent child." Dad laughed and tossed a pair of bundled-up socks my way. I ducked.

"I'm just saying." I swung my legs over the side of the bed and tested my verticalness. So far, so good. Maybe I'd meet Cori and Lainey after all.

"Can I be useful over here?" I grabbed a bunch of T-shirts and added them to the teetering pile on top of my dresser.

"See these things?" Dad smirked and pulled open a drawer. He lined up my socks like little cotton soldiers. "It's a scientific breakthrough. They call it: the drawer."

"Wow. I must have missed that last Obsessive Compulsives Anonymous meeting," I joked.

I helped pick up the rest of the clothes. Soon, only the Michaela tankini was left at the bottom of the laundry basket. We both reached for it at once.

Dad pulled his hand away and smiled. "Good as new." He nodded to the suit.

"Thanks, Dad." I took both pieces and refolded them slowly.

"Your mom would have loved it, by the way." Dad piled the clothes from my hamper into the empty laundry basket.

"You saw the tag?"

Dad straightened and squeezed his eyes shut. He brought his hands to his face and soon, his shoulders shook.

"Oh, Dad. I'm sorry. I should have warned you." I hugged him.

"It's okay…I'm okay." Dad pulled himself together and plucked one of my pink, jasmine-scented tissues from the box on my side table. He blew his nose and forced a smile. "I just haven't been getting much sleep lately."

"That's my fault, sorry."

"It's nobody's fault, just a rough week all round. Hey, you want some breakfast?"

"Thanks, Dad. But if it's okay, I think I might be ready to venture out into the real world again. I'm going to catch up with Cori and Lainey at Bridget's. I could use a bit of girl talk, you know?" I set the bathing suit down at the foot of my bed.

"You really think that's a good idea?" Dad's face hardened into an expression I couldn't read.

"What do you mean?"

"It's just, well, we should decide where we go from here."

"And we will, I just thought if I got to talk to Cori…"

"Jade," Dad interrupted. His voice had an urgency that caught my breath. "Sweetie, you have to listen to me. I don't know what you were planning, but you can't tell *anyone* about what happened the other day. Do you understand?"

"Well, I wasn't planning on taking out a full page ad in the *Port Toulouse Herald*, but…"

"No!"

I flinched.

"I'm sorry." Dad's voice softened. "I'm sure Cori would be a great comfort right now, but it's too risky. No one can know what's happening with you."

I shook my head, trying to understand. "You mean I have to live with this big secret hanging over me?"

Dad paced the room.

"Look." He rubbed his hand through his hair. Again. "This is all new to both of us and without your mom here, we're kind of in a strange place right now. Maybe it'll happen again, maybe not, but if this ever gets out…"

"You mean you think I'll change into a mermaid again?" But I knew the answer from the look on his face. Dad had no idea.

"The only things we know for sure are that Micci was a mermaid and the gene doesn't seem to be recessive."

"No kidding." I fought to keep the edge out of my voice.

"I've been researching this on the web for days, looking for some sort of scientific solution, but I came up with nothing. There must be some precedent, buried deep in the folklore."

"What am I supposed to do until then?" I remembered the promise I'd just made to Cori. Could I really keep lying to her again?

"Let me just do a bit more research to see what I can come up with before we tell anyone. Okay, Jade?"

"But I promise, Cori won't say anything. Not if I swear her to secrecy."

Dad rested a hand on my dresser.

"What you don't understand is if this gets out, your whole life will change."

"More than it has already?" I practically screamed.

"Jade, sweetie." He sighed. "I've worked as an engineer long enough to know that the scientific community would be all over you if they found out. They'd want to explore this phenomenon fully and I'm not ready for that to happen."

My jaw dropped. "Like experiments and lab tests?" A ripple of dread ran through me. Could it be true? Would scientists want to poke and prod at me like some kind of lab rat?

"Maybe. Let's just give this a bit more time before we decide who to confide in. But it's important that you don't tell anyone for now. Not Cori, not your other friends, not even Gran. Please, Jade. You have to promise."

Finally, I could read the expression on Dad's face. It was the same one he'd had when Mom slipped underwater that day at Gran's cottage the summer before. The day both our lives changed forever.

Dad was terrified. And so was I.

"I promise," I whispered.

The reality of the situation slammed into me. This huge, unbelievable thing that had happened could turn into something even more bizarre and horrible if I didn't keep my mouth shut.

"And please," Dad continued, "if anything's bothering you, please talk to me. I'll help any way I can."

Something *had* nagged at me ever since Dad admitted Mom's real identity to me.

"I do have one more question." My voice was barely a whisper.

"What's that?"

"Well, if Mom was once a mermaid…how could she have drowned?"

"Ah, honey." Dad closed his eyes. "That's a question I've asked myself about a hundred million times."

Chapter Seven

I MARCHED DOWN MAIN STREET on my way to Bridget's Diner, my flip-flops flicking to the beat of the cheerleading chant running through my head.

You can do it.

You can do it.

Get on up.

And get down to it...

Not like I was trying out for the pep squad any time soon, but I needed to get my game face on if I wanted to get through lunch without spilling my guts. Dad was right; I couldn't tell anyone what had happened. Not that I didn't trust Cori, but if this secret ever got out, it could change my life forever.

The storefront windows blurred past as I kept my focus straight ahead. A town maintenance guy was watering the flowers, but he stepped off the sidewalk to let me pass. The mounting tempo of my flip-flops must have tipped him off. He obviously recognized a girl on a mission.

I stopped on the bridge at the boat lock to gather my

thoughts and gazed down the mile-long canal from the lake to the ocean, welcoming the warm June sun on my legs.

Ah, legs! Standing upright was highly underrated.

The good news was that I'd *had* legs for four days so far and my first period was now behind me. I'd even managed a couple of showers in the meantime. Dad had waited by the bathroom door, just in case, but I'd been fine. No scales, no fins. Not a gill in sight.

So what was the difference between the shower and the bath? Did a mermaid gene get tripped off when I slipped underwater in the tub? Did it have anything to do with the fact I'd just gotten my first period? Or maybe the Epsom salt triggered something. Dad and I went around and around in circles, trying to figure it out. One thing was for sure: I planned on laying off the Epsom salt even if it *was* the miracle cure for cramps.

I leaned against the bridge's railing and stared into the water. Weird. The ringing in my ears was back. I guess I should have listened to Dad all those times he'd told me to turn down the volume on my MP3 player.

A lungful of ocean air cleared my head. Okay, no use stalling anymore. I stepped off the bridge and headed to Bridget's Diner.

I *could* do this. It was just lunch. I *excelled* at lunch. The waffle fries alone were motivation enough to pull me through.

"Ja…" The ringing in my ears changed and I thought I heard my name.

Was it Cori? Was she running late? I looked up the street. No. Nobody there.

Huh. Well, there was nothing stopping me now. Besides, I'd been stuck in the house long enough. Lunch at Bridget's was just what I needed. I was actually feeling pretty good by the time I stomped up the front steps of the diner.

Until some idiot slammed into me as I reached for the door.

"Hey, watch it!" I yelled.

"Oh, sorry."

My cheeks went from chilled to grilled in about 0.7 seconds when I realized who it was.

"Luke!"

Note to self: refresh supply of moron sticks.

"Jade!" He dropped his skateboard. Right on my toe.

"Sugarplum! Fiddlesticks! Pickle juice!" I channeled all of Gran's semi-satisfying phony curse words to take the edge off the crushing pain.

"Oh, crap!" Luke kneeled to pick up his skateboard and hesitated.

I looked down and cringed. That tail transformation had done a number on my toe nail polish, judging by the Cotton Candy Pink hanging off my nails in chipped bits. And where the heck was my toe ring, anyway?

"I'm so sorry. I, uh…" Luke stood, no doubt stunned by the shocking state of my feet. He hugged his skateboard to his chest to let me by.

"No, no, really, it was my fault," I stammered. "I wasn't watching where I was going." Dissecting the evidence, that was probably closest to the truth.

"Well, I'll own up to the broken toe." Luke held the door for me. "So let's call it even?"

Then, he did it. He smiled that adorable, beaming smile, turning my brain to goo.

"Uh…y'um." *Geesh!* They really should invent a brain implant with a drop-down menu of witty comebacks because right then, I had nothing.

"You going in?" Luke asked, still holding the door.

I worked to engage my gross motor skills, which must have looked strange, because Cori and Lainey glanced up from their booth and stared at me, wide-eyed. I turned to Luke once we were inside the diner.

"Me. Thank you." As soon as the words left my mouth, I gave myself twenty mental lashings.

Pronouns. Must grasp correct use of pronouns.

"You. Welcome," Luke said in his best robotic voice.

I snorted. Not the cute little sniffle-snort Lainey was so good at, but at that point, it didn't seem to matter.

"Oh, and sorry about that 'crap' thing," he continued.

"Next time, try *pickle juice*. It's surprisingly satisfying."

Luke pressed his lips together in a curvy, trying-not-to-laugh smile.

"What?" I asked.

"It's just…" A chuckle escaped from his lips. "Don't take this the wrong way…"

I put a hand on my hip. "Spit it out."

Luke looked at me and seemed to consider what to say. "You're…just different from the last time I remember you."

"Likewise." Ha! Give him a taste of his own medicine.

"Is that good, bad, or indifferent?" he asked.

"I haven't decided yet." I smirked.

Luke laughed. "I guess I deserved that." He waved and continued to the counter to chat with his grandfather, Shaky Eddie, before joining his brother at the booth in the front.

Okay. So maybe Luke wasn't the evil sixth grader I remembered. Even though I was sure I hadn't managed to wow him with my conversational skills, at least he didn't seem to be carrying a grudge over the spin-the-bottle incident. And as long as the Scissor Lips nickname was behind us, maybe it was time for me to bury the hatchet too.

I was still smiling when I slid into Cori and Lainey's booth. "Sorry I'm late."

"What was all *that* about?" Cori whispered.

"You mean Luke?" I jabbed my thumb in his direction.

"Shh, they'll hear us." She poked her head past me. I turned to see what she was looking at. Aha. Luke's older brother sat with his back to the window. He played with a paper-covered straw, his arm draped over the back of the seat.

"Still scoping out Trey, huh?" I nudged her.

Cori blushed and smiled. She turned to her sketchbook and concentrated on shading in the design she'd been working on all spring. A dress. Asymmetric, off the shoulder, and quirky. Just like her.

Lainey pinched her mouth in a sour expression, marring her otherwise perfect face.

"And since when did you become so buddy-buddy with Luke?" The dripping sarcasm in Lainey's voice had me staring back at her, unblinking, for a full three seconds.

"What do you mean?"

"It just looked like you two were having a bit of a moment over there."

"I nearly ran the guy over if that's what you mean. We were just laughing about it."

What the heck was her problem?

"Oh!" Lainey giggled. She turned to flash her Crest Whitening Strip–enhanced smile Luke's way. "Well, that makes sense."

I rewound the last three minutes in my head. How had it seemed to Lainey and Cori, seeing me at the door with Luke like that? Had Lainey actually been jealous? That was a laugh.

I examined the evidence.

Lainey Chamberlain: designer jeans, way-too-cute spaghetti strap tank top, perfectly accessorized, with killer highlights.

Me: scruffy jean skirt, uppermost T-shirt from my teetering pile, and a threadbare hoodie.

Yeah. No wonder Lainey was quaking in her Jimmy Choo knockoffs. As if.

"You gonna have anything?" Cori looked up from her sketchbook. "We already ate."

"Thinking about it." I was grateful for the change of subject. Plus, ever since Cori mentioned the Bridget Burger on the phone, I'd been daydreaming about how many toppings I could get before Bridget started charging me extra. "Are you sticking around for a bit?"

"We'll hang out till you're done. Right, Lainey?"

"What? Oh, Cori!" Lainey tore her eyes away from the window booth for a quarter of a second, then went back to her ogling. "Maybe you can invite Luke and Trey to your pool party."

Whether Luke was buying the serious case of eye batting Lainey was aiming at him or not, I couldn't tell with my back turned. Either way, I had an irresistible urge to reach over and pluck out her plum-tinted eyelashes, one by one, each time she glanced in his direction.

"I'll go order at the counter," I muttered. Two more seconds of Lainey's flirting and I couldn't be responsible for my actions. I took myself over to the swiveling stools and leaned over the cool linoleum counter.

"Hey there, Hurricane Jade." Shaky Eddie looked over from his usual spot at the end of the counter, coffee in hand.

I stared back at him, mouth open. How did he know I was named after a hurricane? I'd just found out a few days before.

I waited for him to take a sip of his coffee.

The mocha liquid quivered in Eddie's cup as he brought

it to his mouth with a trembling hand. Stories ran rampant about his mysterious past. Shell-shocked from a tour in the Gulf? A past career in jack hammering, maybe? From the amount of time he spent at Bridget's counter, drinking coffee while he waited for boats to show up at the lock, I figured he was just a bit over his recommended daily allowance of caffeine.

He put his mug down and swallowed noisily.

"What did you just say?" I asked.

Eddie just smiled. His hand made a rasping sound as he rubbed it over his whiskered face.

"Did you just call me Hurricane Jade?" I continued.

"You always did blow through here like a wind storm." Eddie chuckled.

"Oh." So that's what he'd meant. Nothing more. Or was it? *Forget it*, I told myself. This whole mermaid thing had me paranoid, big time.

"What's good today, Eddie?" I spun the little menu Rolodex and scanned the items.

"Bridget's got those chocolate Wigwags you like." He nodded to the candy rack next to the till. "Or I hear the special's good."

"You just read my mind." It didn't matter that "the special" was the same thing every day. Bridget Burger, waffle fries, and coleslaw (but hold the coleslaw if you want extra fries). I placed my order with Bridget and leaned back against the counter to wait.

Cori and Lainey weren't at the booth. I spotted them

at the door, talking to Luke and Trey. Luke was smiling at something Lainey had just said.

My heart did one of those inside-out numbers, like when you pull off a rubber glove and the fingers get turned the wrong way. What was *that* all about? I wondered. Twenty-four hours before, I thought Luke Martin was the biggest jerk in all of Port Toulouse. So, why did it feel like I just got kicked in the gut, seeing him with Lainey like that?

Cori came over.

"Hey, Luke and Trey are going over to the skate park. You wanna come?" She looked past my shoulder as Bridget set my food on the counter. "Oh, sorry, right."

A quick glance at Lainey, as she tossed her perfect hair over her slim shoulder, and I was reduced to the same self-doubt I'd been plagued with for my almost-fourteen years. Who was I kidding? Of course Luke would go for someone like Lainey. She waved her hand for Cori to come.

"You guys go ahead. Maybe I'll go find you once I'm done."

"You sure? I can wait," Cori said. "Oh! Actually, I'll let them know we'll catch up with them later. That way, we can talk about that thing you mentioned on the phone."

Oh, you mean the fact that your best friend is a half-girl, half-mermaid circus freak?

"Oh, that? It's nothing. Seriously. We'll talk later, okay?" I gave Cori a friendly push and laughed to make sure she wouldn't object. Thankfully, Luke and Trey were already partway out the door with Lainey. "They're leaving. Go!"

"Okay, but make sure you come right over once you're done." She lowered her voice. *"Can you believe Trey actually touched my arm? Eee!"*

I smiled and gave her a thumbs up as she headed outside with the others. I thought I saw Luke glance my way before they all disappeared past the window and out of sight. But no. He probably meant to say good-bye to his grandfather. Or maybe he thought he forgot something.

Shaky Eddie fixed a plastic lid around his takeout coffee and stood to leave. I turned to my lunch and sighed.

"Gotta go, kiddo. I've got another customer." He nodded to the large windows overlooking the boat lock. From the diner's vantage point, I could see the double-masted sailboat cruise up the canal from the ocean to the lake. "Summer rush is starting early this year, looks like."

"See ya, Eddie." I waved.

"Hey. There's a nice bench by the lake near the bridge. Lovely day for a picnic." He winked and planted his hat on his head before disappearing out the door.

"Good idea," I murmured as Bridget came to the register. I nodded to my lunch. "Could I take it to go, please?"

"You got it, honey." Bridget packed up the Styrofoam container and rustled under the counter for a plastic bag.

I turned back to the window and spotted a cell phone left at the Martins' booth. I got it from the table and flicked it open.

fluke1019

"Luke's," I muttered, snapping the phone shut. That must have been why he'd glanced in the diner, like he'd forgotten something. Of course he hadn't been looking at me.

"Just leave it with me." Bridget called over from the short-order window, where she was getting me some plastic cutlery. "I'll keep it at the counter."

"Gladly," I muttered under my breath, placing the cell next to the cash register.

The diner suddenly felt small and suffocating.

I'd practically pushed Cori out the door, avoiding her questions, along with Luke and Lainey. Was this what life was going to be like from now on? Trying to act like a normal teenager while I had this huge secret to hide? Meeting Cori at Bridget's was supposed to make me feel better. Instead, I felt more off-balance than ever. I had to get out of there and sort out a few things.

Bridget returned to the counter and rang up my order. I fished in my pocket for funds and eyed the chocolate-covered caramel Wigwags lined up in their usual spot next to the register and grabbed a box.

"I'm gonna need one of these too."

Chapter Eight

WIGWAGS: CARAMEL AND CHOCOLATE bliss. I leaned back against the park bench and stared out into the lake, savoring the candy's ooey-gooey goodness.

Ah...just what I needed. Kudos to Shaky Eddie for the best idea of the day.

The water in the bay shimmered, reflecting the aspen trees hugging the shoreline. Water trickled from a nearby creek as it spilled into the lake. I kicked off my flip-flops and tossed my hoodie over the back of the bench to get some Vitamin D onto my pasty skin, then closed my eyes so the sun could get a jump on freckle season.

So peaceful. Like the feeling I'd had in that dream the other night, floating in the ocean with the long strands of silk lulling me into a dreamy haze. Pre-tail, that is. Post-tail? *Not* so peaceful.

Wasps buzzed around my lunch leftovers, shaking me from my daze. I sat up and stretched. Just as well. I needed to stay focused. Who knew if the tail thing would happen again? Last thing I needed was to be found flipping around like a marooned trout on the shores of Talisman Lake. I tossed the empty take-out container into the trash so the wasps could have their way with it.

Red lights flashed and a familiar bell clanged, signaling that the bridge was being drawn to let a sailboat through. Boats came from as far away as Florida to sail in our lake. Many headed to resort country near Gran's cottage in Dundee, five miles away, or continued onward for another thirty miles or so to re-enter the ocean through the lake's northern passage.

Shaky Eddie sat up in his control tower puffing on his cigarette, lever in hand. He smiled through curls of smoke and gave me a quick wave.

The lock's large metal gate clunked open, sending a rush of salty ocean water into the freshwater lake. Ribbons of waves danced along the water as the sailboat cruised out of the lock. A couple, about Gran's age, stood on the deck of the boat, looking like they'd stepped out of *Sailor's Quest* magazine with their white pants, blue and white striped shirts, and matching hats. The man stood at the helm as the woman busied herself at the front of the boat, arranging rope into a spiraling coil.

Did the Martins have a boat like that? I wondered. I couldn't imagine living in such a small space for six months. How would I survive without my pillow-top bed and thirty-minute showers? But Luke didn't seem to mind. He even said it wasn't that bad. I thought back to our conversation at Bridget's when he'd told me I seemed different. What did he mean by that? But Luke seemed to have changed too. Did it happen while he was away?

Argh. There Luke was, slipping into my thoughts again. You'd think *transforming into a mermaid* would be the only thing occupying my mind right then. So why couldn't I stop thinking about Luke? Was I actually falling for him?

I shook my head. Even if I was, I had too much going on to obsess over some guy. And I may as well forget about him, especially with Lainey on the scene. That girl had the laws of attraction down to a science. I popped the last Wigwag into my mouth and chucked the empty box into the trash can.

As the sailboat disappeared around the point toward the open lake, another rush of thoughts overwhelmed me. I remembered the last time I *had* been on a boat. My stomach balled up in a tight knot, remembering how Gran's rowboat had shifted below my feet, tipsy and unsure. The memory flashed through my mind like short movie clips.

Me, fumbling with the rope to get it untied from the mooring.

Mom thrashing in the water.

Dad diving in.

Gran yelling into her cell phone at the edge of the dock.

Mom calling for me one last time before she disappeared underwater.

We dove and dove, looking for her. By the time the rescue team managed to maneuver the backcountry roads of Dundee it was too late, too dark, too large a lake. And soon, too many days had passed. I shuddered and shifted on the bench, trying to loosen the memory from my mind.

No wonder I'd had the sweats, trying on bathing suits at the mall. The mere thought of swimming was enough to make me wanna puke. What was I thinking, telling Cori I'd go to her pool party?

I had to do something, go somewhere, and get my mind tracking in another direction. My watch showed 3:40. I should just go, maybe meet the gang at the skate park. But did I really want to put myself through more cringe-worthy chats with Luke? Especially with Lainey there?

I could go home and study. Final exams were just a few weeks away, though my ears had started ringing again and I could really use a nap.

Pillow-top. Nap. Much better idea.

I stood and turned to go, but noticed something splashing in the water, close to the bridge, out of the corner of my eye. A trout? No. Bigger. Maybe a bass. I turned and willed the image to reappear. It reminded me of looking for the first star in the night sky when Mom used to tuck me into bed. There one minute, gone the next.

Splash.

But there it was again. Only this time, a shining flicker of black surfaced for a second then continued underwater, marking its path with a trail of ripples. It moved toward the boat lock as the massive metal gate screeched to a close.

I tugged at my ears as the ringing grew to an annoying

thump like music from a passing car full of high school kids. Meanwhile, two other ribbons of current appeared, twenty feet or so offshore. Trout or bass, all three trails seemed to be on a full-on course for the lock's gate.

The ringing in my ears stepped up a couple of decibels. I winced and kept watch for the flicks and splashes as the fish seemed to congregate below the surface of the water. The gate clunked shut.

Then, a piercing ring impaled my brain with a sound so loud it made me gasp.

"Jade!"

Was Eddie calling from his control tower? Had Cori come looking for me? I looked up, but Eddie was turned the other way, fiddling with something on the console inside his little hut. I glanced through the trees up the bank to the road. The barrier lifted for the cars to cross the bridge, but no Cori.

I turned back to the lake. Something broke the surface of the water. Not a trout. Not a bass. This was much too large.

Dark strands of hair. Pale flesh. I caught the edges of the image. A rubber band tightened around my heart and squeezed with all its might.

"Mom?" My breath sucked in so fiercely, it felt like a spear stabbing through my chest.

Then the image disappeared. I shook my head and covered my mouth with my hand. It couldn't be Mom. Mom was dead. What the heck was wrong with me?

Another splash. The figure returned.

"Jade!" I saw the outline of her perfect mouth hidden behind matted strands of ebony hair. Soon, her whole head broke the surface of the water.

"Mom!"

I ran across the shore, the rough gravel piercing my bare feet. Mom's face dipped in and out of the water. It *was* her! She hadn't drowned! She wasn't dead! I splashed into the lake until I was waist deep.

"I'm here!" A tremor rippled across the water as car tires rumbled across the bridge's metal grating overhead. I reached out for her. "Swim to me!"

Could Mom hear me? Could she see me? I took a few more steps until the water reached my chest.

"Jade…out the…water!" Mom's voice came out as a gurgle as she appeared then disappeared below surface.

"No! Come!" I wasn't getting out. Still, a familiar sense of dread closed in on me. This was the deepest I'd been in the water since the summer before. Even though Mom was there, just a few dozen feet away, the same paralyzing fear gripped me. Then, another terrifying thought crossed my mind. What if I turned into a mermaid again?

My breath quickened. Why wouldn't she just come?

"Swim to me, Mom! I'll get Dad. He's never going to believe…"

But before I could finish my sentence, four hands emerged from the inky water around Mom's head. My whole body shook with terror as the gleaming white fingers reached up and grabbed her.

"No!" I forgot my fears and dove in.

Mom thrashed in the water, tangled in weeds and matted hair. The gnarled, glistening fingers tried to clutch any part of her.

"I'm coming!" I yelled between mouthfuls of water. A rush of heat coursed through my legs as I swam.

"Go back!" Mom called as she bucked and flailed to fight them off.

"I'm almost there!"

But I hadn't even bridged half the distance between us when one of the hands grabbed a fistful of Mom's hair. Her eyes grew wide as her head flew back. She opened her mouth to scream but the sound dissolved in a gurgle as the hands pulled her underwater.

Then she was gone.

"No!"

I treaded water, sculling my hands just below the surface. My eyes darted from side to side for any sign of her—a ripple, a splash, a flicker—anything to give me a clue where she was. But the only thing left was a circle of waves radiating from the spot where the three figures had just disappeared.

"Mom!" I called again, but my voice got lost in the sound of rumbling cars still making their way across the bridge overhead.

I blinked, trying to keep my eyes from blurring over with tears so I could see Mom if she resurfaced. My tongue stung with a familiar taste.

Salt!

I swung my head around. The lock. The salt water from the ocean to the lake. What if it *was* the salt that made me turn into a mermaid? I reached down to my legs and felt for scales forming on my skin, but there was nothing.

Then, something brushed my foot.

"Ah!" I hurled my body toward shore and pulled at the water with all my might.

The thing brushed my foot again and again as I swam, like the feeling of wispy seaweed waving below the surface. But with each kick, the wisps turned into something more solid. Like fingers.

They were after me!

The fingers grasped my ankles.

"No!"

I tried to scream but my mouth filled with water as I was dragged below the surface. My T-shirt billowed around me as I sunk deeper and deeper into the lake. I gagged and gasped for air. But there was no air, just water, everywhere around me and inside me. It shot past my throat to my lungs, forcing a fizz of bubbles from my mouth.

A big, red panic button tripped off in my brain. Was I drowning? What about Mom? I needed to get to her. What about Dad? Losing us both would destroy him!

Air! I needed air!

Without thinking, I inhaled a gulp of water as I struggled to get away from the vice-like grip around my ankles. I braced myself to gag, but amazingly, the suffocating feeling disappeared. What should have been a relief turned to a sickening horror as I reached for my legs and felt the uneven scales forming on my skin. My thighs began to fuse.

Not again!

I tried to kick the feeling away but suddenly, I heard a ripping sound and a humongous blast shot me through the water, forcing the hands to let go.

My hair swirled around my face as I landed against the bottom of the lake. A cloud of dirt kicked up from the lake floor, making it hard to see. I could tell I still had my shirt and skirt on, so I was pretty sure the ripping sound came from the familiar white bits of cloth floating up to the lake's surface. Sure enough, the dust cleared and my granny panties were gone, along with my legs.

In their place? A disgusting, slimy tail.

No! The sound of my voice rang all around me.

This couldn't be happening! I didn't want to be a mermaid. I didn't know *how* to be a mermaid. I could barely remember how to swim. But I couldn't waste time freaking out. I had to find Mom and escape from this whacked-out underwater world!

I searched around, trying to get my bearings. The water was tinted a murky brown like the color of old tea. It tasted worse as it passed through my mouth with each breath. Of water! How was that even possible?

The surface of the lake loomed high overhead. I could make out the boat lock's large metal gate a few dozen feet away. Fish darted in and out of clumps of swaying reeds. A rusted bicycle, partly covered in green algae, rested at the bottom of the lake.

Mom and the scary-handed water freaks, though, were nowhere in sight. Where did they go?

My body bobbed in the flowing current of the lake. I hung on to a large rock and wiggled the tail to keep from being swept away. The ringing in my ears was still there but it seemed more like a mixture of sounds, each with its own tone, like a group of people talking at a party.

Something moved near the bicycle. My whole body tensed as my eyesight adjusted to the surroundings. A face. An arm. A tail. Piece by piece, a mermaid's body materialized from the mossy rocks and swaying reeds.

But not Mom.

A few feet away, closer to the lock, the same thing happened. This time a merman. I turned and saw more of them. One by one, like a massive underwater game of *Where's Waldo*, mer-people appeared all around me. Four…seven…eleven, maybe? They huddled in groups, sneaking glances at me, whispering in the same annoying ring I'd been hearing, off and on, for the past few days.

Holy crap!

Gran's phony curse words just weren't cutting it this time. First of all, I was sporting a tail at the bottom of a lake, *breathing water*. Plus, I was surrounded by mythical aquatic creatures and had a sinking feeling I was just about to become shark bait!

But Mom?!

Where is she?! My voice came out as a ring too, like I'd tuned into some kind of mer frequency. Was this how they communicated? Obviously I'd need a Mermish/English universal translator, because no one seemed to understand me judging by the glazed over looks I was getting.

That's when I saw him.

The ugliest, meanest looking merman on the face of the planet. (Though, I looked working from the shallow end of the gene pool.) His face looked like soggy bread, covered with a scraggly beard. Beside him, another mermaid had Mom by the hair and was dragging her away. Mom turned her head toward me.

Stop! My voice rang out. I let go of the rock and wriggled the tail to try to swim her way.

Ugly sneered and screeched a series of rings, setting the group into action. The mer-dudes broke from their huddles and began to roll large rocks along the bottom of the lake toward the base of the boat lock's metal gate. Ugly grasped a large rock and heaved it onto the growing pile.

What were they doing? Were they trying to block the lock from opening?

I turned back to Mom and whipped the tail to go faster. Ugly motioned for two other mermen and nodded at me. Mom rang back a sound I didn't understand. The mermen hesitated, but Ugly raised another rock toward them. He was obviously the alpha-male of the joint because the mermen snapped to attention and swam my way.

I flicked the tail to the right to try to avoid them and kept heading for Mom, but they caught up to me in seconds, making my pathetic attempt at swimming look like the mermaid doggie paddle. One of them grabbed my arm and spun me around, scratching my face in the process. I swung my free hand and connected with something I hoped was a jaw.

Hiss…

Someone didn't like that. He grasped my wrists.

Ugly laughed.

Things kind of went downhill from there.

Chapter Nine

M Y SCALP ACHED FROM being dragged through the lake by Ugly's henchman. What was it with those guys and *hair*? They shoved me into a creek a short swim away and stood guard while Ugly and another mermaid waved the other rubbernecking mer-dudes back to the rock pile. Obviously, they didn't want an audience for whatever brand of torture they were planning.

I cowered behind a submerged moss-covered log and tried to catch my breath, which, underwater, was a completely different skill set compared to breathing air. Plus, the fresh water in the creek seemed thin and suffocating, like trying to breathe at the top of a mountain.

Ugly jabbered away at the mouth of the creek, barking at the others. What were they planning to do? Kill me? Stuff me like a brook trout so they could hang me over their mantle like a fishing trophy?

I looked down at the tail, still attached to my lower half. It flicked back and forth in the flowing water, as involuntary as blinking. Even when I worked to keep it still, a small shift in the current set it off again. How had this disgusting thing become so much a part of me in such a short amount of time? I didn't want this. I never wanted this! But I was beyond freaking out. Seeing Mom being yanked away like that had transformed my shock into a desperate fear. I needed to figure out a way to help her!

I turned, trying to get my bearings. The water in the creek was only a couple of feet deep. I could make out a hill, sloping upward, through the rippling water. The bridge was about a hundred feet away, past clumps of brush lining the bank. I must have been in the creek Cori and I had waded through a million times when we were little, looking for pollywogs.

I eyed the bank a short swim away. It would hurt like crazy, but maybe I could crawl out of the water and escape. The tail would transform back into legs, wouldn't it? I could run and get Dad. But then, how would I ever find Mom again?

What had they done with her anyway?

Seconds later, my question was answered. A huge wave surged toward me and I saw them heave Mom into the creek. She sunk like a rag doll.

*Mom…*I gasped and pulled her into a hug. My hand tangled in her hair and I drank in her smell, expecting the peach scent of her shampoo. Instead, the water around her tasted like an aquarium left too long between cleanings, her skin felt swollen and uneven. I shrunk back, without thinking, and instantly regretted it. *I'm sorry. I'm so sorry…*

*Shh…*Mom put a finger to her lips. She nodded to the

three mermen and mermaid at the mouth of the creek as they screeched at each other in rings and tones.

Ugly looked our way for a second. He took the mermaid by the arm and swam away, out of earshot, no doubt to plot our demise. His henchmen piled branches and rocks at the creek's opening to block us in.

I can't believe you've been alive all this time! I blurted, once they'd moved away from the mer-made dam. My heart still hadn't settled from the shock of seeing her. *I thought…me and Dad thought…*

Oh, Jade. Mom hugged me, but her arms were weak and limp. *I missed you so much.*

Can they understand what we're saying? I stole a glance past the dam.

Mom shook her head. *No, but we don't have much time. They're planning to move us farther up the lake.*

Are you okay?

Mom's cheekbones jutted out over her sunken cheeks. Her eyes sagged in the corners. But she was still beautiful. Always beautiful.

I'll be okay. She smiled weakly. *But you?*

Mom, how can this be real? How can I be breathing underwater like this, talking to you? Speaking in rings and tones felt like Spanish class. How could Mom even understand what I was saying?

Jade…I never meant for them to do this to you…

She reached out and took my hand but each word was heavy with effort.

Who are those jerks? I whispered. *That ugly guy and the mermaid…did they do this to you?*

That's Finalin and his wife, Medora. The others just do as they're told. Mom stroked my face. *Oh, Jade. There's so much I need to tell you before they come back.*

I tugged her arm. *Well, they're not here right now. Let's just crawl out of the water, sprout legs, and make a break for it. I'll call Dad. We'll take you home.*

Mom pulled me back. *No, Jade. I can't do that.*

Her words stabbed through my heart.

Yes, you can. My tears were immediate. Though, crying underwater probably lost a bit of its effect. *It hurts like crazy, but that's what happened to me the other night when I was a mermaid for the first time.*

Mom brought a hand to her mouth. *You've changed before? That must be why you finally heard me today. I've been calling your name for months, each time I saw you cross the bridge.*

I remembered the ringing in my ears and hearing my name earlier that day.

That was you!

Yes! Mom replied. *What happened when you changed?*

I thought of all the things that had led to the transformation. I told her about the Epsom salt and getting my first period and how I'd fallen asleep in the bath tub and slipped underwater.

Oh, Jade. Mom stroked my arm. *I wish I could have been there to help. How did Dad take it?*

Actually, he was really cool about it, I said quietly.

And you were able to change back? Mom's face seemed to reflect five different feelings at once: happiness, sadness, regret, fear, and maybe a teensy bit of hope. I couldn't let that hope fade away.

At first we thought it was the salt, but I think it has something to do with breathing air or water. What I can't figure out is; why now? It's not like it's the first time I ever swallowed water. What about the time I almost drowned at that hotel in Ottawa?

I remembered how the chlorine had stung my throat as I tried to find the surface, so far above me. I finally struggled to the side of the pool, gagging and gasping for air. Mom dragged me out. I'd hurled.

Oh, Jade. Mom continued stroking my arm. *Your first period must have triggered it and the salt may have given everything a boost, but you're right: breathing air or water forces the change back and forth. That's what happened when I first became human. I changed back when Finalin and Medora pulled me underwater last summer.*

I could hear their high-pitched rings on the other side of the dam.

They did this to you? My fear turned into a seething, ugly hatred. *But Dad told me it was the Mermish Council that let you become human in the first place. Why did they change their minds?*

Mom looked past the dam and shook her head. *Finalin and Medora aren't part of the Mermish Council. The Council lives out in the ocean with the rest of the mer-world. Those mers out there are inmates. The Council uses Talisman Lake as a prison.*

I remembered the screeching sound of the large metal gates of the boat lock. My whole body shivered with the truth. *You mean, they're criminals?*

Mom nodded. *They call themselves Freshies. And believe me, there's no way I would have set foot in this lake if I had known the Council was locking up criminals behind the boat lock. Especially with* my *toes.*

That's when it clicked. I gasped. *Our webbed toes? That's how they knew?*

Mom nodded. *Every mer hears the story of the Webbed Ones growing up, but none of us ever believed that becoming human was possible. I didn't, until it happened to me. And now, Finalin and Medora are determined to get the secret out of me.*

So they can break out of here? I could only imagine the havoc *that* would cause in Port Toulouse.

I can't blame them. Fresh water is no place for a mer, Mom said. *That's why most of the Freshies hang out by the lock where the salty ocean water spills in. Finalin and Medora have been here the longest so they've had a few more years to get used to it. It's much harder for us though, especially if they move us farther up the lake where the water is fresher.*

I couldn't stand to see the strain of the past year in the thinness of Mom's arms and the dark circles under her eyes. I had to get her out of there. I swam to the creek bank.

So let's escape while we can!

Jade, wait! Mom rang out and grabbed my hand. She brushed my hair back. *It's different for me. I didn't start off being human, like you. I can be out of the water for a little bit at a time, but I can't just crawl out. If it were that easy, all those guys out there would be walking around town by now.*

But how did *you finally become human?* I asked.

There's a tidal pool on the ocean side. Mom motioned through the water to the bridge. *The tides in the pool kept me in and out of the water, breathing air and water for the right combination of time to make the change safely. Otherwise, I'd suffocate. The tidal pool is the only way.*

I tried to line everything up in my head, but it didn't come close to seeming real. *And earlier…when the lock was open…you were trying to escape to the ocean to find it…*

Yes. I've been waiting all winter for the lock to reopen.

And then I came and ruined things… The possibility of Mom ever becoming human again seemed to get farther and farther away from me.

Someone began to pull back the branches from the dam.

It was a long shot anyway. Mom spoke quickly, keeping an eye on the mouth of the creek. *No one has ever gotten past the armed sentries at the end of the canal. But I thought if I could just talk to them…tell them how I got in here…*

Finalin's voice rang out.

What's he saying? I whispered.

Seems your arrival has kicked things into high gear. He's more determined than ever to find out my secret. That's why they're piling rocks to block the boat lock, so we won't try to escape. She sagged in the water, exhausted.

I'd made things worse. I should have stayed out of the water like Mom asked. But then, how would I have finally seen her and made sure she was safe?

More rocks and branches disappeared from the top of the dam. We shrank back.

Just tell me where the pool is! Dad and I will find it and come back to get you.

Mom pulled me close and shook her head. *The Council blindfolded me; I have no idea where it is.*

Try, Mom! You must have walked away from the pool afterward. Was it near anything?

Mom closed her eyes. *I'm sorry, Jade. I wasn't in the best shape when it was all over.*

It was no use. She didn't remember. *So I'll just stay here with you.* I clung to her as more of the dam got pulled away. *We'll figure out how to escape together.*

Jade, listen to me. It won't do us any good if we're both captured. You need to get out of here! Mom pushed me toward the creek's bank with more force than I thought she could muster.

I can't just leave you!

Finalin and Medora's heads appeared over the shrinking pile of rocks and branches.

You have to! She shoved me up the bank. *Go, Jade. Tell Dad I'm okay and that I love him. I love you too!*

My face broke the surface of the water.

"No!" I wailed. But the sound came out with a mouthful of water. My lungs sucked back a breath. I panted, shocked by the air burning its way through my lungs, sick at the thought of leaving Mom behind.

Go! Mom's voice rang through the water. She was right. I was more help to her on land than in there. I'd get Dad. Together we'd figure out how to rescue her!

Sharp stones pierced the skin of my elbows as I heaved myself up the creek's bank. My fingernails dug into the earth as I grabbed at the roots to pull myself up. Something connected with the tail I dragged behind me. I whipped it up, out of the water and rolled onto dry land. A hand lunged for me again and again, but by then I'd managed to work my way up the bank, out of reach, beside a patch of bushes. I looked back to the water. Whatever had been chasing me flipped back and disappeared with a splash.

But Mom. Where was she? Was she okay?

I collapsed against a mound of dirt as the scales on the tail glistened and began to glow. The pain grabbed hold and clenched my body with a powerful force. The agony didn't creep up on me with a warning like it had the time before. This time, it came all at once, in one huge, body-wracking, breath-robbing, skin-searing wallop.

"Mom…" I gasped. My whole body shook with sobs.

I tried to look back to the creek, wishing I could just roll back into the water to be with her no matter what, but I couldn't tell up from down or left from right as my head spun with swirling images.

The water, the ugly hands, the screeching metal lock, the swaying reeds, the rocks, the branches.

The pain...the horrible, terrifying, mind numbing pain...

That must have been when I passed out.

Chapter Ten

I WOKE UP SHIVERING.

Every cell in my body screamed as I sat up and pulled my knees to my chest.

Knees! That was good sign. I shook with a mixture of cold and relief. No tail, no scales, just my normal, beautiful, pudgy knees and stubbly legs in desperate need of shaving.

The bridge drew long shadows across the inky depths of Talisman Lake. A cool evening wind swept up the canal from the ocean, transforming the aspens lining the lakeshore into trembling shadow-makers.

How long was I passed out? I wondered. Long enough for my T-shirt and jean skirt to dry into crunchy, stiff versions of their former selves, apparently. But, just as I expected, my underwear was gone. This mermaid thing could wreak havoc on a girl's wardrobe.

I struggled to my feet and pulled on my hoodie, welcoming its warmth, and tried to remember the string of events that had me down for the count behind a couple of scruffy bushes by the creek. That's when the terrifying memory of hands emerging from the water cleared the brain fog from my thoughts.

"Mom…" I rasped.

I shivered and stumbled over rocks and tree roots, trying to follow the creek as the bushes scraped my legs. A powerful waft of fried foods attacked my nostrils. I must have been getting close to Bridget's Diner.

"Mom?" I strained my ears to hear over the noise of the trees and passing cars but the ringing sound was gone. My head spun with questions. If the ring was gone, did that mean Mom was gone too? I ran up and down the creek, but she wasn't there. Where had they taken her?

My throat burned. I must have swallowed a gallon of water because the inside of my stomach roiled like a snake trying to escape from a burlap sack.

"Au-augh…" The snake escaped. All over the ground.

Ew.

Waffle fries and Wigwags did *not* make such a great combination in their semi-digested state. I spit the bitterness that hung on my tongue and wiped my mouth on the sleeve of my hoodie, then stumbled to the base of the bridge to find my flip-flops near the bench where I'd kicked them off earlier. I looked back to the bushes by the creek. What if someone had found me there?

My hands shook as I pulled my cell from the pocket of my skirt to call Dad. I jabbed the buttons. Nothing. The water must have killed the phone when I was in the lake. What was I supposed to do now?

I hugged myself and looked up to the bridge. The streetlights were already lit. A lone car meandered across, heading downtown. Pedestrians strolled along Main Street past the bridge, looking in the shop windows. A couple entered the thrift shop like it was just another Saturday in Port Toulouse.

But this wasn't just any old day. Something had happened. Something important. My mom was alive! Though what would anyone think if they found me along the shores of Talisman Lake screaming about my dead mother? I could imagine all the billable hours it would take Dr. Becker to deal with that!

I needed to get to a phone to call Dad. He was going to go nuts when he found out what just happened. I scrambled up the bank to the road. Cars pulled into the parking lot at Bridget's. Could it be the dinner rush already? Was it really that late?

"Hiya, Jade." Bridget looked up from a table full of customers as I pushed through the door of the diner. I must have looked as wrecked as I felt, cause her face went from its usual cheery expression to creased concerned. "You okay, hon?"

"Yeah, I'm fine." I waved and hurried to the dark hallway that led to the restrooms where an old pay phone hung on the wall. My whole body shook from cold and shock. I fished into the pocket of my jean skirt and found some change.

One ring. Two rings. Why wasn't Dad home? I hung

up after the fifth ring before the machine picked up and jammed the quarters back in the slot to try his cell. Maybe he popped out to Home Depot for his latest DIY project. I checked my watch. The glass pane blurred with a fine mist. Geesh. I *knew* no good ever came from swimming. First my cell, now my watch. My whole repertoire of personal technology was now soggier than a three day-old diaper.

Pick up, Dad, pick up! I willed him to answer his cell but I knew chances were slim due to Engineer rule #1. If Dad couldn't walk and chew gum at the same time, how did I expect him to drive and talk on the phone? I left a message.

"Dad." I glanced around the diner to make sure no one heard. "I'm at Bridget's. You're never going to believe what just happened." I lowered my voice as much as I dared. "It's Mom. She's alive. She's in Talisman Lake. Just come quick, okay?"

I hung up and rested my head against the cool molded plastic of the pay phone. My useless watch clicked-clicked, ticking off the same second over and over. Seconds lost without Mom. Would we ever see her again?

Headlights flashed across the diner's back wall as a car turned into the parking lot.

"Dad?" I turned to the window.

Pickup truck. Not Dad. Plus, Dad had yellow fog lights. I'd laughed when he told me he'd paid $280 to get the safety lights installed, especially when he insisted on using them even on clear days. But the yellow lights were nowhere in sight.

The sun hung low over the ocean bay at the end of the canal. Half an hour, tops, and it would be dark. Should I go back to the lake to try to find Mom myself? Scary mer-dudes or not, going back to the lake was the only thing left to do without Dad there.

I tied my hoodie around my waist for extra security, given that I was going commando under my skirt, thanks to my wardrobe malfunction back in Talisman Lake. Once I'd managed to arrange my scraggly hair around my face, I walked back out into the diner.

Oh. Shaky Eddie.

I'd been on such a mission to get to a phone, I'd missed him on the way in. He sat at his usual spot, trembling mug of coffee in hand. He glanced my way. His eyes squinted in a smile as he brought the mug to his lips. I forced a smile back and tightened the hoodie around my waist, but something niggled at me. What would have happened if I hadn't seen Eddie there earlier? I would never have gone to the lake like he'd suggested.

I would never have seen Mom.

Then it hit me. The hoodie! I'd put it on the bench at the base of the bridge. How did it get draped over me, a hundred feet away by the creek where I'd passed out? The only person who knew I was down there was Eddie. Had he…

"Jade! Where were you?"

"Oh!" I jumped and turned to see Cori enter the diner with Lainey at her side. Luke and Trey hung back, deep in conversation.

"Don't tell me you've been here this whole time?"

"Hi, uh, me? No...I went home." I worked to get my heart back into my chest cavity as my head swirled with thoughts.

"Why didn't you come over to the skate park?" Cori brought a hand up to my cheek. "What happened to your face?"

The scratch from the mer-jerk. I reached for her hand and pulled it down, laughing.

"Ha-ha. You know me. I can be such a dork." I needed to come up with an excuse. Something believable. Something quick. Not like I could admit I just spent the last couple of hours, out cold, beside Talisman Lake recovering from tail-like symptoms.

Think. Think.

"I just...well, I had to catch up on studying." Weak. I pulled at my damp hair, trying to pad my story. "Then I grabbed a shower and I guess I was still a bit woozy from being sick all week because I slipped in the tub and whacked my face on the towel bar. Brutal, huh?"

I could feel my nerve endings fray with each lie. I felt like pond scum, misleading Cori like that. This was worse than the Lie. This was the Lie to End All Lies.

"Aw, that's too bad. You gonna be okay?" Cori asked.

"Oh, yeah. I'm fine." But I wasn't fine. I was standing in the middle of Bridget's Diner, trying to find my dad because my mom was being held captive by criminal mer-people at the bottom of Talisman Lake.

I was anything but fine.

Lainey let out an impatient sigh and flicked her hair over her shoulder to glance back at Luke. She turned and looked me over. I caught a glimpse of a sneer. No doubt she'd noticed that I had the same clothes on as earlier, pre-supposed-shower. I hoped there weren't mud or grass stains to give me away.

"Well, we missed you," Cori continued. "And, oh, skateboarding gave me the best idea! I was thinking I could design a whole skater kind of look. What do you think?" She moved her hands side to side and narrowed her eyes like she was attacking a half pipe. "Kind of an edgy, urban-chic skater vibe?"

"You could definitely pull it off with those fierce moves." I laughed, but meanwhile I wondered how I could put an end to our conversation and get out of there. Every minute spent talking meant another minute lost trying to find Mom. Plus, I had to talk to Eddie. I stole a glance at the counter. It was empty. Where did he go?

I caught Trey giving Luke a warning kind of glance when they looked up from their conversation. What was that all about?

"Well, we've gotta bounce, so see you guys later!" Trey gave Luke a brotherly jab to the arm. "Come on, bro."

"You mind walking me home, Luke?" Lainey followed and grasped his arm. She turned back. "You coming, Cori?"

Finally. Even though I still felt the urge to pluck out Lainey's eyelashes, I could feel my whole body sigh.

"I dunno," Cori said. "What about you, Jade? You wanna come over to my house?"

"Oh, no thanks! I'm gonna head home."

"You sure?" she asked quietly.

"Yeah. My dad's picking me up." I looked past her, through the window. The streetlights spanning the bridge were already lit. Was Dad on his way home? Should I try him on his cell again?

"Hey." Cori gave me a nudge. "Feel better, 'kay?" she whispered and gave me a quick hug. I smiled to try to reassure her, but her eyes searched my face. I could tell she knew something was up, though I doubted "mermaid" and "risen from the dead" were on her radar.

"I'm fine. Don't worry." Another lie. They piled one on top of another in an ugly heap. I caught a glimpse of Luke as they all turned for the door. His face had an expression that was hard to read. Did he think I was being a flake, blowing them off twice in one day? Could he see through me too?

Oh, I should tell him about his cell...but he was gone. Again.

I couldn't think of that just then. I couldn't think of Dad driving somewhere along the streets of Port Toulouse, his message light flashing on his cell, or of Cori heading home, worried about her best friend. I couldn't wonder why Eddie disappeared or imagine Luke and Lainey walking off into the sunset.

And I definitely could not waste one more second

standing in the middle of Bridget's Diner while Mom was lost in the vast expanses of Talisman Lake.

It was dark by the time I made it back to the lake. Aspen leaves shook all around me like rattling maracas as I walked along the shoreline, guided by the light of the bridge's streetlamps.

I stuffed my hands under my armpits to warm them and called over the lake, not daring to yell in case people from the street could hear.

"Mom...Mom..." Was she there, waiting for me to come back? I watched for any ripples or splashes, careful not to get too close to the water. Maybe they were all still there, watching me, just under the surface of the water. Would the Freshies come after me again? I shrank back at the thought. No way was I setting one duck-webbed tippy-toe in *that* lake any time soon.

Cars rumbled over the bridge on their way home for dinner but Dad's yellow fog lights were still missing along the road. I pulled branches out of my way to check the creek one more time. Still empty. Mom was gone. Long gone.

I sank to the ground against a moss-covered rock and felt a new wave of sobs collecting in my chest. Why didn't I stay with her to help fight off those guys when I had a chance? I buried my face in my hands and let the tears flow. Sure *I* was safe, but what did that matter if Mom was still in there, somewhere, with Finalin and Medora making her life miserable?

Would I ever find her? Would we ever get her back home? I stood and wiped my eyes with the back of my hand. Dad's yellow fog lights turned on to Main Street.

"Dad!" I stumbled through the alders, past the park bench, and up the incline to the guardrail skirting the road.

"Dad!!" I yelled again, waving my arm high in the air.

His car passed by Bridget's and headed toward the bridge. Could he see me? I moved closer to the streetlamp and waved.

"Daddy!"

He looked up and rammed on the brakes. The tires skidded and clinked gravel against the metal guardrail. Dad put on his hazard lights and jumped out of the car.

"What? What is it, Jade? Why are you out here all by yourself?" He reached for me and hugged me. "Are you crying?"

"Didn't you get my message?"

"What message?" Dad pulled his cell from his pocket. "Oh, sorry. I must have had the music on too loud. What's the matter?"

I looked up into his eyes. He didn't know. He had no idea Mom was still alive. That she'd been living in the lake all this time. That I'd found her and hugged her and talked to her.

Then abandoned her.

And now, I had to tell him.

Chapter Eleven

HOW MANY TEARS CAN you cry before your body gets squeezed dry?

I felt completely wrung out by the time Dad and I arrived home well past midnight after combing the banks of Talisman Lake for Mom. Nothing. Not a ring in my ears. Not a trace that she'd been there in the first place. I was seriously beginning to question my sanity.

Dad promised to stay with me until I fell asleep.

"You believe me, don't you?" I asked into the darkness of my bedroom.

He reached out from the chair next to my bed and found my hand.

"Of course I do," he whispered.

"She said to tell you she loves you." My face screwed up as I remembered the last words Mom called out before forcing me out of the water.

"I know, honey. We'll find her. I promise." But from the way the outline of Dad's shoulders shook in the low light of the window, I wondered if we ever would.

The next morning, Main Street looked like it had been covered in a shroud of grey. A fine mist hung in the air, smelling of damp ocean seaweed. I greeted Cori in front of Bridget's on the way to school.

"Hey." I handed her a hot chocolate, a Monday morning ritual.

"Hey, yourself, sunshine. You like?" Cori breezed past me. Her hair was stacked high on top of her head like a model from *Real Runway*. She wore a version of the asymmetrical dress from her sketchbook.

"You finished it!" I reached out and felt the silk material between my fingertips. That expression about something taking your breath away was really true, because I could barely manage the next few words. "It's awesome..."

"Lainey's mom wants me to come by her studio this afternoon to show her. I figured I'd get some mileage out of it in the meantime."

"She's gonna love it."

"Hope so!" Cori flipped back the plastic top from her hot chocolate's lid. She took a sip and winced. "Hey, I thought it was my turn to treat. I was even going to get my free one from Mug Glug's." She dug into her satchel and fished out her Frequent Sipper card.

"Save your freebie. We'll celebrate at Mug Glug's when Mrs. Chamberlain signs you up for next year's co-op term."

I took a drink and sucked in my cheeks at the bitter taste. Yeah, Mug Glug's would have been a better choice. Bridget's Diner may have been the waffle fry capital of the world, but their hot chocolate wasn't going to win any Reader's Choice Awards in the *Port Toulouse Herald*.

But I hadn't dropped into Bridget's for their hot beverage selection. I needed to see Eddie to try to figure out if he knew anything about Mom. When I got there though, he still wasn't at the counter. Strange, considering the guy had permanent butt impressions on that stool of his.

"I think he decided to take a few days off while the lock is closed for maintenance," Bridget had said when I asked where he was.

"Maintenance?"

"Yeah, Eddie had to turn a boat away earlier this morning when the motor blew on the controls as he tried to open the lock. They've got a crew out there right now, trying to figure out why the gate won't open."

So the stacks of rocks the mers had piled up against the lock had worked! Though, I was pretty sure "Mermish Sabotage" wouldn't be one of the options on the maintenance crew report.

"How long will the lock be closed, you think?" How would Mom ever get back to the ocean if her only exit was blocked? And how long could the mers keep up the blockade?

Bridget didn't know, but sure enough, the sound of rumbling trucks and heavy equipment pierced through the cool June morning air as we headed toward school.

Cori took another sip and fell in step with me. "Don't take this the wrong way, but you look like you got run over by that truck back there."

"Thanks." I slapped her arm with my free hand. "I feel like the crud between the tire treads, so I guess that qualifies."

"Hey, I tried you on your cell last night, but I couldn't get through so I left a message at your house. Why didn't you call me back?" Cori asked.

"Oh, my cell is toast and we got in really late…had to drive to Gran's to help fix her air-conditioner." I stared straight ahead and tried to shake the lie from my voice. "Then she made us dinner…" I was laying it on a little thick "…by the time we got home, it was way too late to call back. Sorry." I blew on the hot chocolate and took a careful sip, hoping that part of the conversation was over.

"I wanted to tell you about the music I downloaded. I thought we could do this whole Caribbean theme, you know?" Cori swayed her hips, holding her hot chocolate like she was sipping cool iced tea on a far away beach.

"For what?" I snuck one last glance at Talisman Lake before it disappeared behind Main Street's buildings.

"For my pool party!" Cori grasped my arm. "You're still coming right?"

"Um."

Crap. Pool party. This new mermaid development might put a kink in those plans.

Cori was quiet for a few steps. Then she tugged gently on my arm and turned me toward her.

"What's going on with you, Jade? It's like we're not even on the same wavelength anymore."

"I, uh." What could I say?

"Are you mad at me or something?" Cori searched my face.

"No. No! Of course not."

"Because it doesn't seem like you're that into the pool party anymore. I thought after we found that bathing suit..."

Bathing suit—period—bath—mermaid—Mom.

The thoughts connected in my head like beads on a string. Then I remembered the white stitching with Mom's name on the tag, making the connection from bathing suit to Mom far closer. The memory set off a flare inside me.

"I've gotta go." Before I knew it, I shrugged Cori's hand away and took off down Main Street. Hot chocolate sloshed from my cup, burning my hand.

"Where are you going?!" Cori called.

I turned, not long enough for Cori to see the tears streaking down my face. I knew if I stayed with her one more second I'd spill my guts. I ached to tell her everything just to have one more person in the world understand what I was going through. But I remembered the promise I'd made to Dad. If the truth ever got out, who knew where that would lead?

"I forgot! I told Higgins I'd help set up for Sports Day!"

Lie. Lie. Lie.

"Jade!"

The lies chased me past Mug Glug's, past the post office, past the blurring images of Main Street, nipping at me like rabid dogs. Running away would solve my problem for now, but it didn't change the fact that I was part mermaid, my mom was alive, and that she was being held captive by an underwater lake monster and his posse of aquatic barbarians.

How could I continue being Cori's best friend if I had to keep hiding my deepest, darkest secrets from her?

The sun had burned off the morning dew by the time I reached the sports field. A whistle blew farther downfield, urging a gym class through a series of punishing-looking soccer drills. Mr. Higgins was all too happy for the extra help, though he seemed a bit surprised by my sudden enthusiasm for relay games. He dropped a mesh bag full of balls next to the Gatorade table and untied the bag's drawstring.

"I wasn't aware you were so invested in sports, Jade. You know, we always need girls for the field hockey team. Or, better yet, have you ever thought of water polo?" He poured the balls on the grass and bunched the bag into his hands.

Water polo. I snorted.

"Oh, sorry. I'm usually not much of a joiner. Just trying to do my good deed for the day. This counts for community credits, right?"

Higgins sighed and started back toward the school for the next load of gym-inspired torture devices. "Just bring your credit form to the office for me to sign," he called over his shoulder.

"Water polo," I muttered as I grabbed a stack of pylons and started setting up the obstacle course. "As if."

"Hey!" Someone called from behind.

"Ah!" I stumbled back, tripping over one of the pylons.

"Whoa!" Warm arms wrapped around me to keep me from falling. The scent of sunscreen and gym class enveloped me in a not-unpleasant way.

"Luke." I turned in his arms, surprised by how close he was. Heat rose in my cheeks. I looked up into his crystal blue eyes, framed with impossibly long eyelashes. The early June sun cascaded off the sheen of his cheeks…

"I hope you have good accident insurance." Luke laughed. He let go and stooped to pick up his sports bottle that had fallen to the ground.

"Well, ahem…" I turned off the *Sweet Valley High* soundtrack in my brain and met his gaze as he straightened from retrieving his bottle. "You're going to have to come up with a better M.O. than knocking me over every time you want to say hi."

"Hey, you should be thanking me. I just rescued you from a pylon injury."

"Well, if you're playing the dashing young hero angle, you should really shower first." I waved a hand across my face, but couldn't help smiling.

"If you think this is bad, don't go near the guys' locker room after gym class. It would curl your toes." Luke got a strange look on his face then busied himself at the Gatorade table, refilling his bottle.

"Do you get many girls wandering into the boys' locker room?"

Luke snapped the top of his sports bottle shut and laughed. "Sadly, no."

"Poor you." I patted his shoulder, a gesture which, in more expert hands, might pass as flirting. But that was Lainey's department, not mine, so it wasn't like I had anything to lose.

"Hey, I keep meaning to ask you; did you lose this?" Luke fumbled in his pocket and held out a strip of crumpled paper. "It must have gotten mixed up with my stuff at Dooley's."

I took the paper in my hands and unfolded it.

Michaela 2-piece/Swimwear $76.99.

The receipt from Hyde's. Instant tear alert. What was it with this bathing suit?

"Um, yeah. Thanks."

"'Cause I figured you might need it. The receipt, I mean. The bathing suit too, I guess." He took a swig of Gatorade.

Blink. Blink.

"Thanks." I peeled my eyes off Mom's name and stuffed the paper in my pocket. "Oh, did you get your phone back?"

Luke pulled out his phone, flicked it open, then snapped it shut.

"So, fluke1019, huh?" I asked. "Is there a story behind that?"

"You saw that, huh?" Luke looked at me for a moment

then smiled. "There is a story, but you wouldn't believe me if I told you."

I laughed. "Secret double agent for the French Foreign Legion? Deep cover for the KGB?"

"Close." Luke smiled and shoved the phone back in his pocket. "So, do you swim much?"

"Hate swimming."

Luke laughed.

I put a hand on my hip. "Well, that's nice. I might have a paralyzing water phobia for all you know and all you can do is laugh?" It was meant as a joke, but one obviously lost on Luke.

His face fell. He started to talk and stopped a few times before managing a sentence.

"Sorry, that was really stupid of me. I just thought…" He stared at the ground and jammed his toe into the turf like he was trying to loosen the dirt from the bottom of his running shoe. "I heard about what happened to your mom last summer," he added quietly.

Me and my big fat mouth! Of course he'd feel bad about that, even though it was the first time in a year I hadn't connected swimming with Mom's supposed drowning. Why did I have to choose that precise moment to have a lapse in memory? And why, why, why didn't I have those idiot filters replaced between my brain and my mouth during my last moron tune-up?

"No, no. I was just joking." I caught his eye. "Hey, listen. The sooner you embrace your inner klutz and the sooner you understand what a smart mouth *I* am, the better. Let's just stop apologizing to each other for our glaring shortcomings, okay?"

Luke looked at me with his curvy lip, trying-not-to-smile smile and extended his hand.

"Deal."

We shook on it.

"But no more talk about swimming or bathing suits or anything aquatic, okay? Makes me wanna barf."

"Got it. But do sailboats qualify? 'Cause, my family always does this end-of-school boating trip to D'Escousse. Wanna come?"

All my brain filters unclogged spontaneously. My neurons snapped to attention. The fact that Luke was inviting me on a boat cruise registered on boy-girl level, but something else clicked too.

"When?!"

"Last day of school. It's early dismissal that day so we'll probably leave around lunchtime. That's if they have the lock fixed by then."

That was it! If I knew exactly when their boat was going through the lock, I might be able to get Mom safely to the ocean. Then she could find the tidal pool to help her transform into a human again. Then, she could come home. Of course, I'd have to find her first, but I would. I had to. And hopefully, the Freshies would have run out of rocks by then. But how could I help Mom and be on the boat at the same time?

Think, think…

"So, like a boat cruise?" I filled in the dead air, hoping to buy time so I could sort things out in my head.

"A boat cruise!" Lainey pranced over, appearing out of *nowhere*, sporting a jewel beaded crop top and spotless white capris. Cori followed, talking to Trey. She didn't look my way. I can't say I blamed her. Lainey grasped Luke's arm. "That sounds like so much fun. I can't wait!"

I'm sure the visible tremor working through my body must have looked like I had some sort of neurological disorder, but I couldn't help it. How did she do it? How did Lainey Chamberlain manage to include herself in every conversation where Luke Martin was concerned?

Unless Luke had already invited her too…

"Yeah, should be a blast," Trey added. "We're going to pick up our cousin, Stewart, in D'Escousse. Jade, you coming?"

"Uh…" I did the connect-the-dots on the group dynamics.

Cori and Trey.

Lainey and Luke.

Me and some cousin named Stewart from D'Escousse.

Pity date.

Idiot.

I turned, trying to hide the burning fire in my cheeks. In my usual graceful manner, I bumped the nearby table, toppled over the Gatorade cooler, and sent it careening onto the ground. The top of the cooler popped off and I watched in silent horror as a fountain of orange liquid sprayed everyone within a ten-mile radius.

"Ah!" Lainey's hands flew up. She looked down at her white capris, now bedazzled in Technicolor orange. "Great. Just great! Good one, Jade. And look what you did to Cori's dress!"

Cori's dress! The outfit she'd been working on all spring! It was now splattered in a spray of orange specks as well.

"Oh, no! I'm sorry. I'm so sorry…"

Of all the times in my life to be a klutz, this had to be the worst.

"It's okay," Cori whispered.

"No…here. Let me help you." I searched the table for a roll of paper towels and ripped off a large brown strip. "I'm such a jerk. I wasn't looking…" I dabbed Cori's dress, my heart in my throat.

"Really. Don't worry about it." But Cori's voice was tight and small.

"Don't pat it!!" Lainey brushed my hand away. "You'll crush the fibers. This is going to need a special stain remover. We'll take it to Mother's dry cleaner." She took Cori by the shoulders and led her back to the school. Her voice rang across the school yard, a hundred times more piercing than Finalin or Medora's screeches.

Dad would say that every action has an equal and opposite reaction and this was no different. I turned the other way and ran off the field, head down, mumbling apologies.

As I brushed past Luke I thought I heard him mumble something too.

"I guess I'll take that as a no?"

Chapter Twelve

To her credit, Cori called and left a message. I called back and left another. The whole situation went all sideways and as days turned into weeks, it got harder and harder to say anything without looking like a big jerk for letting so much time slip by.

The Great Wall of Lainey didn't help with her snide comments and withering looks. Plus, the long nights spent with Dad, combing the banks of Talisman Lake for Mom, didn't put me in the best mood for relationship building.

So, between the Great Gatorade Fiasco and Mom disappearing, a huge gaping hole grew in my heart, threatening to bust wide open.

The only good news was that I managed to last three weeks as a two-legged, land-dwelling mammal. The bad news was that the boat lock was still closed (though Dad had gently suggested they dredge some of the rocks out of the lake to avoid another "rock slide"), Shaky Eddie was still on vacation, exams were looming, and I'd barely had time to study.

"English tomorrow?" Dad asked one evening.

I looked up from my study notes and took another bite of grilled cheese. With ketchup. And a chaser of grape soda. Dinner of champions.

"Mm-hmph," I mumbled and nodded to the leather-bound book opened at Dad's spot. "Whatcha reading?"

He flipped the book closed for me to see.

I swallowed.

"Mermaidia: Fact or Fiction?"

"I special-ordered it from Copenhagen."

Dad stifled a yawn. I knew he returned to the lake every night once he thought I was asleep. His yellow fog lights caught the reflection of the disco ball hanging from the curtain rod in my bedroom window, sending shards of dancing light across the darkened walls. Each night while he was gone, I lay awake, listening for his key in the door, his footstep on the bottom squeaky stair, and the soft whoosh of the office door next to my room. It wasn't until I heard the whirr of the computer booting up before I was finally able to fall into a body-numbing sleep.

Dad pushed the book toward me and went to the fridge to get milk for his granola. Another complete and balanced meal.

"Did you find anything good?" I leafed through the raw-edged pages of the book.

"A few interesting tidbits, but I'm finding it hard to make heads or tails of it all."

"Heads or *tails*?" I asked, rolling my eyes.

"Oh, ha!" Dad returned to the table and sat down with a satisfied smile. "I can be quite clever when I'm not trying."

I took another bite of grilled cheese and flipped through to the middle section with the photos and illustrations, but the pictures were hand drawn in pen and ink and were really weird looking.

"Is this what people think mers look like?" Snake-like hair, three pronged spear thingies, and webbed hands? Sheesh. One merman looked like he was throwing a sailboat across the water. A mermaid seemed to be luring a human into the water. I leafed through the rest of the book but stopped when a chapter heading made my breath catch short. "Oh!"

"What?"

I pointed to the words: *The Webbed Ones.*

"Like what Mom told you about?" Dad pulled his chair closer.

I nodded and began to read the page-long excerpt.

"There is a large body of evidence suggesting that humans descended from pre-historic aquatic mammals or Pesco-sapiens."

"See?" Dad tapped the page. "There's that word again. I don't just make this stuff up, you know."

I smiled and continued reading.

"The human body supports this theory. Human hair is found in lesser quantities than that of their ape counterparts and is arranged toward the midline of the body. This works to reduce aquatic drag. Humans also have a descended larynx like that of a seal, making it possible to regulate breathing while diving and surfacing..."

I turned to Dad.

"It all kind of makes sense, doesn't it?"

Dad wiped his hand on a napkin and pulled the book toward himself to read on. There was a part about how some of the pre-historic Pesco-sapiens may have kept evolving in the water while humans evolved on land.

"It says that small populations of aquatic Pesco-sapiens are believed to exist throughout the world."

"But how do they *know* all this?" I asked.

"Wait a sec." Dad brought a spoonful of cereal to his mouth and mumbled as he scanned the page. "Here's a medical report of a *Webbed One* from the Liverpool Psychiatric Hospital. It's dated 1908." He pointed, farther down the page.

I read the passage aloud.

"A 38 year-old male, rescued from a near-fatal cliff dive, insisted he was attempting to 'return to the sea.' The patient identified himself as a 'Webbed One' claiming his webbed third and fourth toes were proof that he had transformed from a 'merman' to a human. The subject required restraint to prevent further harm to his person. After extensive psychiatric evaluation, he continued to maintain his story, elaborating that the transformation had taken many weeks of breathing a combination of air and water in a magical tidal pool. The patient could not pinpoint the location of the tidal pool, citing amnesia. After extensive shock and drug therapy, the patient spent his remaining days in a catatonic state."

I turned to Dad.

"They just locked him up like he was crazy, didn't they?" I said quietly.

Dad nodded and covered my hand with his. "His story *was* pretty unbelievable, when you think of it."

"But *we* know it's true. The same thing happened to Mom! All of it is true." I fanned through the pages. Then I caught another sight of the webbed hands and the airborne boats. "Well, maybe not *all* of it."

Dad rose and took our dishes to the sink. He ran the faucet and squirted a stream of dish soap into the steaming water. "I'm getting the feeling the title says it all."

I slammed the book shut. *Mermaidia: Fact or Fiction?*

"So they just jammed a bunch of mermish trivia together and we're left to figure out what's real and what's fake?"

"It probably took years to compile all this data, but it would be impossible to verify it in any substantial scientific way." Dad took a scrub brush to the frying pan.

"If only they had actual proof in here. Something else to go on." I sat back in my chair and folded my arms across my chest.

Dad shook his wet hands over the sink. "Oh, I remember reading something about a supposed mermaid discovery back in the '80s or '90s. Maybe that'll shed some light." He wiped his hands on a dish towel and returned to the table, then turned to the index at the back of the book and ran a finger down the rows of text. "Where was that?"

"An actual mermaid?" I leaned forward and rested my elbows on the table to have a look. "Why is this the first time we ever hear about it?"

"Well, if the Mermish Code of Silence I've been

researching is true, it seems mer-people are very good at keeping their identity a secret."

"Who can blame them after what happened to that poor guy." I wondered if the man from the hospital had felt as alone with his secret as I did with mine. Was that why he felt like he had to tell someone? But what did that get him other than a one-way ticket to the looney bin? Dad had been right: no good would ever come from revealing this part of me.

"Where was that thing…" Dad kept flipping through the pages. "Oh, here, under *Witness Accounts.*

"Mermaid remains were reportedly found in the Gulf of Mexico, 1991. No physical evidence is available to authenticate these claims, though a scientific study was presented by Dr. E. Schroemenger. (Pesco-Sapien: Myth or Fact? Journal of Marine Biology, 1992, Vol. 32.*) The report was later dismissed as anecdotal."*

"Everyone probably thought that Schroemenger guy was a kook too." I took one last sip of soda and crushed the can in my grip.

"Yeah, but maybe he wasn't such a kook after all. In fact, maybe I could pay him a visit on my way back from my Finite Element Analysis conference in Dallas." Dad studied the book. "It looks like he was based in Florida."

"You're still going to Dallas?" My soda can clattered onto the table.

"Jade, we talked about this. I need to go to this conference to present my paper on integrated theories of flow dynamics."

I went to my happy place until he was done talking about the merits of unified fluid theories.

"...you'll stay with Gran. And I checked with Mrs. Blake for the night of Cori's pool party."

Not like I was going.

"But what about Mom?"

"I've been meaning to talk to you about that." Dad paused and shut the book. He placed his hands on the table and exhaled a long, deep breath. "I don't need to tell you how rough these past couple of weeks have been. This trip is probably just what we need right now. If we still haven't made any progress finding Mom by the time I leave, it might be a good chance to take a bit of a break from looking."

"Stop looking?" My jaw slackened. I blinked several times, not quite believing what he'd just said. My mind flashed back to the summer before, when the Search and Rescue guys had said the same thing. But that was when we thought there was no hope for a person who'd sunk to the bottom of the lake. Now we had proof that Mom was alive. How could Dad even think of giving up?

"Not stop"—Dad ran his hand across the book's leather cover, his eyes downcast—"but I think we should take a step back and get a bit of perspective. At least until I can do more research."

"You can't be serious."

"Honey, it's been almost a month and all we've got are dead ends." Dad took off his glasses and pinched the bridge of his nose. "Of course we're going to keep looking but I'm worried about you, Jade. Cori hasn't been around for weeks, plus neither of us is getting any sleep. And the guys at the office have been working overtime to help me prepare for this presentation."

"But what if something happens while you're gone?"

"That's why I got you this." Dad reached into his briefcase and pulled out a new cell phone. "My number's programmed in there. You can call me if anything comes up. Even if it's just to talk."

He pushed the phone across the table toward me. Any other day, a new cell would have been awesome, but just then I had the urge to throw the thing across the kitchen.

"But Dallas?" He may as well have said Neptune.

"Aw, sweetie." Dad rested his hand on my forearm. "I would do anything to find Mom, you know that, but we can't keep putting our lives on hold. You know Mom wouldn't want that." His voice grew quiet. "And if this Mermish Code thing about protecting their identity is true, there may come a time when we have to accept the fact that we might never find her."

My whole body fired at once.

"No! You don't know that!" I shrugged his hand away and stood, toppling my chair onto the floor behind me. "We *will* find her. We just…"

Dad stood too and pulled me into a hug.

"Mom has to come home." I murmured, wetting the cotton of his shirt with my tears. "She just has to…"

Chapter Thirteen

THE CORI SITUATION SEEMED to take one step forward and two steps back. I'd managed to sit with her in the cafeteria one day without a Lainey audience. The conversation started out well enough.

"So you and Trey seem to be getting along well," I began.

"Yeah." Cori poked her salad with a plastic fork. She looked up and I think I caught a teensy bit of a smile. Good start. "He's really amazing. We all went to the beach party on Saturday. I wish you could have been there."

And yes, she'd invited me. There was a message. But my nights had become a bit occupied.

"Luke brought his guitar and Lainey kept wanting to sing 'Kumbaya.' It was so funny."

I must have had a physical reaction to Lainey's name because Cori dropped her fork into her bowl and stared at me.

"You don't like her, do you?" Cori held my gaze.

"It's not that, it's just…" How could I describe what I was thinking without sounding petty? And to be fair, I hadn't said anything to Cori about my feelings for Luke. I wasn't even sure how I felt about him myself. But Luke aside, Lainey and Cori actually had a lot in common. They both loved fashion and I knew how important Mrs. Chamberlain's mentorship was to Cori. I couldn't begrudge her of that.

"Because," Cori continued, "I hope you know who I'd pick if it came down to a choice between you and Lainey."

This wasn't the conversation I'd meant to have. The plan was to sit down, lead in with some casual banter and finish up with a heartfelt apology about ruining her dress. How had things gotten so off track?

"Did I hear someone say my name?" Lainey flounced over with her cafeteria tray and installed herself between Cori and me. She adjusted an oversized coat over her shoulders and prattled on about how cold it had been at the beach party and wasn't it sweet of Luke to loan her his jacket?

End of conversation.

And I hadn't even gotten to the part where I apologized.

End-of-school exams passed with a blur. Somehow, I'd banked enough points during the school year to get me through, but just barely. It must have been those extra community credits from Sports Day.

Dad's Dallas trip arrived without any sign of Mom and my desperate optimism turned into a ticked off feeling I didn't like. Of course it was irrational, it wasn't like Mom stood a chance against Finalin and his crew, but the whole thing got all confusing and weird and everything became Mom's fault. My trouble with Cori, my crappy grades, it all got mixed up with the fact that if Mom had just figured out a way to escape from the Freshies while I'd gone to get Dad, everything would be on its way to becoming normal again.

I imagined Mom waiting for me at home every day, ready to help me study or to sort out the Cori/Luke/Lainey thing over milk and a plate of cookies. And since it was my fantasy, I made the cookies oatmeal chocolate chip.

Not like Mom was ever the baking-cookies-type, and unfortunately, Gran wasn't exactly Susie Homemaker either. Dad dropped me off at her cottage in Dundee on his way to the airport just in time for dinner. I punched the numbers on the microwave keypad to zap my frozen entrée.

"Watch out for the steam when you peel the plastic wrap off the dish, Jadie. Those suckers will rip the skin right off your fingers, I tell ya."

Gran's cottage embodied lakeside living with its low ceilings and faux paneled walls. The tiny vintage kitchen had barely enough room for the two of us, given the fact that I'd inherited her "pleasantly plump personality" as she liked to put it. I guess I had to inherit *something* from Dad's side of the family, though I would have settled for the Baxter family's genius-level brain power. It might have saved me a bit of final exam angst.

"Thanks, Gran. Oh, the Salisbury steak, huh? Looks yummy."

It wasn't Gran's fault that Dad had bailed on me and left me there so I did my best to keep the mood light. But it was a struggle, as the black tray limped around the microwave's turntable while steam collected on the glass door.

"My pleasure. I'm just so happy you're here. It gets lonesome up in this part of Talisman Lake without all those Jet Skis and the late night carousing."

Gran wasn't exactly a "commune with nature" kind of gal. The only reason she lived so far north was for the easy access to the local casino where she could apply her keen, analytical mind to managing thirty Bingo cards at once.

I rolled my eyes. "You don't fool me. I bet Mr. Whitehouse is keeping the car warm at the end of the driveway so you can make your getaway. Isn't Thursday night Winner-Take-All?"

She giggled and patted my arm.

"Well, I worry about how your dad is coping with a teenager in the house. You need any new bras, Jadie? Oh, is that deodorant I got you working out okay?"

Morbid embarrassment set in.

"Yes, Gran. It's fine," I muttered.

After dinner, Gran offered to stay and watch movies with me, but I knew the jackpot had been building for six weeks so I convinced her to go. It would be nice to have a bit of time to myself and Gran's rubber arm was easily twisted.

"Only if you're sure," Gran called out from the passenger window as Mr. Whitehouse's car pealed out of the driveway in a cloud of dust.

I waved good-bye and went back to the kitchen to raid the pantry for ingredients to make my standby chocolate fix: Chocolate Mug Cake. The Salisbury steak just hadn't cut it and with no Wigwags in sight, I was desperate. I spooned the cocoa powder, sugar, flour, and other ingredients in my mug and zapped it in the microwave for five minutes. When the bell dinged, I grabbed a tea towel to pull out the mug of steaming chocolate cake, drinking in the sweet scent.

Bliss!

I plopped a spoonful of vanilla ice cream on top and went to sit on a deck chair down on the dock with the massive, dog-eared *Mermaidia* book tucked under my arm. I'd read almost the whole thing since Dad brought it home during exams, which may have explained my pathetic grades.

After reading through the last fifty pages of mind-numbing mermaid trivia, and under the effects of my current chocolate buzz, I decided a couple of things must be true:

1. Whoever put that book together probably wasn't much fun at parties.
2. The mer/human evolution thing had to be true. Along with the larynx and hair thing, some other stuff cropped up as I read.
   - Humans have an extra insulating layer of fat, perfect for swimming. (Big checkmark in that box from me!)
   - Our salty tears and sweat probably meant we had

been ocean-dwellers at one time, just like Mom had said.

- Human sweat may act as a waterproofing system.
- And some other stuff about hooded noses and *vernix caseosas* that I had no clue about.

3. And the *Webbed One* stuff was definitely true, since Mom was the one who'd mentioned it in the first place. Some stuff I wasn't so sure of:

4. I hadn't decided if that Schroemenger guy was a kook or not, but maybe Dad's trip would uncover the truth.

5. Did any of this matter if we never found Mom again?

I shut the book and looked out over the water. Dundee may have only been five miles north of Port Toulouse but Talisman Lake looked totally different here. Instead of the narrow bay by the boat lock, the water was about two miles across in this area. Cottages dotted the shorelines of several islands a short boat ride away. Others poked out along the lakeside amid the crooked pines and granite landscape.

For an evening in late June, the lake was unbelievably quiet. But that would soon change since the only thing standing in the way of summer was the next day's school-end reports. I considered skipping the whole thing and calling the school secretary to fake a deadly wood tick bite or porcupine attack, but I'd chickened out.

Thankfully, it was a morning dismissal since it was the last day, plus, faking a deadly wood tick bite might raise suspicion.

I could make out the whirr of a Jet Ski farther down the

lake. Sounded like someone was getting a jump on summer after all.

Lucky them.

I scraped the last bit of cake from the bottom of the mug with my spoon, contemplating what the summer had in store for me. But a whole summer without Mom or my best friend bordered on unbearable.

I hated to admit it but maybe Dad was right. Maybe it *was* time to take the pause button off life and start making plans. No amount of obsessing would bring Mom back, but I *could* do something about the Cori situation. Yes, the conversation in the cafeteria hadn't gone so well, but I should at least give it one last shot.

I set my mug down and fished my new cell phone from the pocket of my hoodie, then dialed Cori's number before I could change my mind.

"Cori?"

"Jade."

Was it too late to apologize?

"Um, we didn't really get a chance to finish talking the other day. I was wondering if we could meet at Mug Glug's after school tomorrow. I'd really like to see you." I'd keep the apologies for when I could do it properly, face to face.

"Yeah, sure. I think I could swing that."

Easy as that.

"Okay, see you tomorrow." We said our good-byes and I clicked the phone closed.

Huh. That wasn't as bad as I'd built it up to be in my

imaginary obsessive world. I'd just apologize and offer to pay for the dry cleaning. Anything to make up for my super loser Gatorade maneuver.

Did it make me a bad person if I hoped Lainey didn't show up? Either way, I wasn't going to let Lainey Chamberlain get in the way of apologizing to Cori this time.

I leaned forward in my chair and gazed down the lake past the islands to see if I could spot the Jet Ski coming around the bend. Maybe it was the Hendersons from the next cove. Or maybe the Beckers were already at their island cottage. Dr. Becker's daughter, Chelse, went to private school and usually got out a week early.

Yep. The Beckers *were* here. A plume of smoke curled up from their chimney and I could see their canoe tied up at their access dock next to Gran's property.

Oh! Maybe Chelse would teach me how to use their Jet Ski this year.

The excitement about learning to Jet Ski caught me off guard, but between that and meeting Cori to look forward to, I was already feeling more hopeful than I had been for the last few weeks combined.

Whoever *was* on the Jet Ski didn't seem to be getting any closer though. In fact, its engine just whirred steadily, without the usual revving sounds Jet Skis made when they sped up and slowed down.

Although…was that a whirr or a ring?

Chapter Fourteen

THE MUG AND SPOON clattered onto the deck as I sprung from the deck chair and raced to find the boat shed's key under the rubber mat by the door.

I jammed the key into the lock as my thoughts raced with memories of doing the same thing with Mom every summer when we'd go for our middle-of-the-lake rides in the rowboat. But this wasn't one of those lazy July afternoons with nothing to worry about but reapplying sun block and wondering what Dad was burning on the barbecue.

If that sound was what I thought it was though, maybe we'd see those days again.

I ran inside and pressed the buttons for the boat lift and the overhead door. Pinkish-orange light from the setting sun flooded through the boathouse as the garage door opened. The rowboat traveled down from the rafters along rattling chains and settled into the water. I scrambled in, unhooked the pulleys to release it from the lift and grabbed the oars.

The boat shot out of the shed with three massive strokes of the oars. I felt like some superhuman she-force, driven by the massive dose of adrenaline gushing through my veins. In that moment, I was sure I could lift a car off a family of four or save a kitten from a burning building. And if Mom was out there, I would find her, rescue her from those scary mer-dudes and bring her home.

Once the boat neared the first group of islands, I let it drift. Water dripped from the oars in plinking drops, so I pulled them inside to listen.

Yes. The ringing. It was still there. It was louder.

"Row, row, row your boat…" I sang as loud as I dared, hoping Mom would hear. I couldn't very well shout out her name.

A screen door slammed shut from the direction of the Beckers' island cottage. The squeak of a pulley carried across the water. Someone must have been hanging laundry on the clothesline.

"Gently down the stream…" Dr. Becker would book me for a whole new round of head shrinking if she figured out what I was trying to do. I really didn't want to spend another four months "getting in touch with my grieving" and "verbalizing my pain."

"Merrily, merrily, merrily, merrily…" I drew the rowboat near the Becker's island, following the ringing sound. I dipped the oars into the water just enough to hug the island's shore. Thankfully, the crooked pines bowed over the water, keeping me well hidden from the cottage at the top of the steep hill. The ringing grew as I approached the dock.

"Mom?" I whispered.

A wave emerged from within the dock's crib. Was that just the current from the rowboat reflecting back toward me?

"Mom?" I tried again.

I glanced up to the cottage. The screen door slammed again. Hopefully, whoever was hanging laundry had gone inside.

Waves continued to fan out from within the dock. Was Mom under there? I pulled the oars in and caught the side of the dock with my hand. The ringing in my ears was deafening. I tried to channel the noise into a word, like we'd done a couple of weeks before.

Mom, if you can hear me, tell me where you are.

I waited. I thought I heard something, then the word was gone. Was it really a word or was I just willing it to happen? Then, finally, I heard it again.

Here…

Mom! I ducked my head and peeked under the dock. The sun caught the green glint of the scales on her tail. It was Mom! Really Mom! My whole body sighed in relief. But there was another feeling too. One that surprised me.

I went back to the creek with Dad and you were gone! The words came out harsher than I intended.

It reminded me of the time Mom lost me at the mall. She'd yelled at me to never leave her side again before suffocating me with hugs and kisses.

Exactly like that.

Only this wasn't the mall with a kind security guard

feeding me lollipops. And just like Mom had done at the mall after chewing me out, I broke down, crying with relief.

Mom lifted her hand through the water. *No…so… sorry…* But her arm slackened at her side before she could finish her sentence. Was she hurt?

I jumped from the boat to get closer and shivered as the water met my chest. Then I saw Mom through the water. All of her.

Her body lay like a wet towel on the rocks, lining the bottom of the dock. Her eyes were dark pits against her almost transparent complexion. Blue veins ran in random cords along her arms.

Ohmigod! Are you okay? My anger turned upside down. *What did they do to you?*

Mom didn't answer. Then I remembered. The water. I licked a wet finger. It was completely fresh. How long had she been stuck here, without salt?

I grasped the rowboat before it began to drift away.

Wait here. I tied the boat's bowline to one of the crooked pines close to shore and stole a glance at the cottage. Who was up there? They probably couldn't hear us since we were speaking in rings, but if anyone caught me, what would I say?

What would Dad say? Oh, crap. My cell phone. I pulled it out from the pocket of my hoodie and flipped it open. Damp, but still functional.

Ja…

I tossed the phone on the boat's seat and rushed back to the dock. I'd call Dad as soon as Mom was safe.

I'm coming! I rang.

But I couldn't get to her. Logs spanned across the dock's wooden supports. Well, not exactly logs, but fallen trees with snapped off branches.

Trapped. Mom managed to say.

They'd locked her in.

How long have you been in here?

She lifted her hand and held up three fingers. It was obvious from the look on her face and the slowness of her movements; it hadn't been three hours or three days.

Ever since the day in the creek?

She nodded.

That upside-down anger for the Freshies turned to full-on spitting nails with a side order of lethal poison darts. How could they do this to her?

Where are those idiots? I rang out the words and clawed at the logs. *I swear: if I ever get my hands on them, I'll rip their hairy arms off!*

I pulled with all my strength, but the logs didn't budge. I waded around the dock and tried from the other side but Mom's dock prison was rock solid.

*Hunting...back soon...*Mom tried to lift her head to warn me.

Don't worry. I splashed back to the rowboat and grabbed an oar. A door creaked from the direction of the cottage and slammed shut. Was someone coming? I pushed the boat under the cover of the pines and ducked under the dock with the oar. I had to move fast.

*No…Jade…*Mom shook her head.

I'm not leaving you again!

Mom's eyelids fluttered as she struggled to stay conscious. *Jade…the Freshies…not long…*The ring of her voice disappeared along the current of the water.

This isn't going to take long.

I plunged the oar underwater to wedge it between the logs and forced it down. The log budged an inch, then shifted back into place.

I'm getting you out of here.

Grunt.

Then I'm taking you to the ocean.

Urgh.

The oar flexed under my weight. Thanks to my love of waffle fries, Wigwags, and Chocolate Mug Cake, the log shifted.

Then you're going to become human again and come home.

The log pulled free and tumbled to the bottom of the lake, barely missing my foot. I reached in and grabbed Mom to yank her out into the open lake.

And if those hairy-armed mer-morons have anything to say about it, they'll have to go through me!

Mom managed a feeble smile and let herself be carried along, too weak from her weeks in fresh water to resist even if she wanted to. Was I too late? Could she even make the trip to the ocean?

Step one. I'd get her to the boathouse.

Can you swim to Gran's? But I already knew the answer. Mom shook her head from underneath the water.

I couldn't pull her into the boat. She was barely conscious already; there was no way she'd survive outside of the water. Maybe I could tow her to the boathouse with the bowline. If I rowed backward, it might work!

Here, so you don't get chafed. I pulled off my hoodie and reached underwater to get Mom's arms through the sleeves. Once the rope was around her chest I splashed back to the dock to get the oar.

Oh! And call Dad. I needed to call Dad.

A twig cracked.

"Jade! I *thought* that was you."

"Dr. Becker!" My head shot up. I whacked it against the dock.

"Oh, are you okay?" Her hand flew up to her head. She winced. Probably some kind of head-shrinking, mirroring technique.

"Yeah." I rubbed my head and crawled out from under the dock. "Totally fine." But inside, I was panicking, big time. How long had Dr. Becker been standing there? Did she know something was up? Could she see the outline of Mom's mermaid body under the water?

I held up the oar. "I, er, just lost this overboard and it drifted over here. Hope you don't mind."

"Not at all, in fact, I'm happy you're here. How have you been?"

I waded back to the rowboat, avoiding her gaze.

"Oh, just hunky dory! Peachy keen, that's me."

Dr. Becker laughed and walked the last few steps to the shore. I straightened the boat to hide Mom as she floated underwater on the other side.

"Well, it's lovely to see you."

"Yeah, it's nice to see you too." I pasted a smile on my face and waded to the middle of the boat to climb in. Hopefully Mom was okay and the rope would hold while I towed her to the mainland. "I'll just head on back to Gran's now!"

"Jade, wait!" Dr. Becker called after me.

I froze. Did she know what was going on?

I turned slowly. "Yes?"

"I was just wondering…"

Wondering what? If I was trying to hide the existence of my mermaid mother from a clinical psychologist? Surely, that had to qualify me for one of the more serious mood disorders.

"…if you could you give me a lift to my car on the mainland."

Phew.

"Sure!"

Gah! Why had I just agreed to that?

Dr. Becker smiled and started for the seat in the stern. I was so preoccupied with the thought of hiding my cargo that I shoved the boat into the water and started rowing before she even had a chance to sit down.

"Whoa!" Dr. Becker caught herself against the side of the rowboat and settled into her seat.

"Hang on, it's gonna be a rough ride!" I joked as I rowed toward the Beckers' access dock next to Gran's cottage, towing Mom from the bowline.

"Why are you rowing backward?" Dr. Becker asked, in her probing, therapist, "let's explore this behavior" kind of way.

"Oh, I just like to mix things up a little. Forward, backward…I'd row sideways if I could." Rambling. A sure sign of mental instability.

She craned her neck to look over my shoulder. "Your bowline is dragging."

Don't look. Don't look. Don't look.

I needed to turn this conversation around.

"You're a bit of a rule follower aren't you, Dr. Becker?" I narrowed my eyes as I continued rowing. "Is that a behavior you'd care to explore?"

Dr. Becker laughed. "I guess you got me on that one. Here you are, doing me a favor, and all I can do is badger you." She chatted about how Chelse brought her boyfriend up for a visit and how they'd taken the canoe, leaving her stranded, and how Mr. Becker wasn't back from the marina with the speedboat yet. "So, thanks for the lift," she continued.

I turned to check the bowline and noticed a flicker of splashes near the dock we'd just left behind. Were the Freshies back? I rowed faster, putting my back into it. Maybe it was the crazed, furtive glances I was stealing from the dock to the bowline to Gran's boathouse, but all of a sudden, Dr. Becker stopped talking and stared at me.

"Are you sure everything is okay?" she asked. "You seem distracted."

"Me? No…" The rowboat approached the mainland shore. "…watch yourself, coming in for a landing!"

Dr. Becker's head snapped back as the boat ran aground, stern first, near their dock. Her hands flew to the sides of the boat to brace herself. "Oh! That was quite a boat ride."

If those were the Freshies back at the Beckers' dock, I needed to hurry and ditch the shrink to get Mom to the boat shed safely. Especially since the sun was starting to disappear behind the trees.

Dr. Becker stepped out of the boat and straightened. "Ah yes, there's the canoe. And just great, now the car's gone."

While Dr. Becker grumbled something about having to walk to the marina to catch up with her husband before it got too dark, I imagined Mom drifting below the water, and the Freshies poking around the island looking for her. This was not good.

"Well, have a great evening!" I called out, maybe a bit too eagerly.

Dr. Becker turned and studied me for a moment before speaking. "Before I go, is there something you'd like to share? You just seem a bit…well, scattered today."

Scattered? Um, yeah. But despite the fact that Mom looked very weak and that the Freshies were probably on the hunt already, I couldn't stop the warm, hopeful feeling growing in my chest.

"I'm totally fine!" I made no effort to hide the crazed smile plastered across my face.

"Because, if you're feeling out of sorts, we could always resume our sessions."

No amount of therapy could undo the fact that I believed I was towing my undead mermaid mother on the bowline to keep her safe from rogue mer-criminals. But, as far as I was concerned, Mom was finally on her way home. If that made me crazy, I was probably beyond help.

"Don't worry about me, doc. I've never felt better."

Chapter Fifteen

"C AN YOU HEAR ME if I talk normally like this?" I untied the rope from Mom's chest and climbed up onto
the boat shed's dock to shut the overhead door and turn on
the light.

Mom nodded. Her eyes drooped with exhaustion.

"Just rest. Everything's gonna be okay."

Then it hit me like a Slurpee brain freeze. *Would* everything be okay? I hadn't thought past getting Mom to Gran's
boathouse. Now I was in No Man's Land.

How would I get Mom from Dundee to the Port Toulouse
boat lock, and who knew if the lock was even open? What
would I say to Gran in the meantime? And, ugh, there was
no way I could meet Cori at Mug Glug's tomorrow, given
this new development. But at least I didn't have to fake a
deadly wood tick bite to miss the last day of school.

Last day of school! The boat cruise!

I reached over into the rowboat to get my cell.

fluke1019

I couldn't believe I was texting him.

hurricanejade: hi l…boat cruz still on?

My phone lay quiet for three agonizing minutes.

fluke1019: tmrw @ 12…u in?

The lock MUST be reopened. Maybe the maintenance foreman had finally listened to Dad and started pulling rocks out of the lake.

hurricanejade: gr8. see u @ lox if i can come. ttyl! ☺

"Yes!" I snapped the phone shut.

Mom poked her head out of the water for a second. "Good news?"

"There's a sailboat going through the lock tomorrow at noon. Hey, I didn't know you could talk with your head out of the water like that."

"For a few minutes…so the Freshies can't hear…but Port Toulouse…so far…"

Good point. How was I going to get her to the boat lock? Especially since the only person in on our little secret was probably on a plane to Dallas by now. I checked my watch. Dad's plane took off at about nine p.m. Oh! Maybe he got delayed.

"I'm going to try Dad." After four rings, I left a message.

"Dad! I found Mom. We're here at Gran's cottage. Call me as soon as you get this message."

Mom's face emerged from under the water. "No?"

"He must have had to turn off his cell on the airplane."

"Can't stay here." She nodded to the garage door. "Freshies…looking for me…"

I looked through the water and saw what she saw. The light from inside the boathouse peeked out from under the garage door into the inky water. The mer-dudes could just swim right under the door and find us.

I turned off the light.

"I need to get you out of the lake."

"Need water…no use…" Mom had given up.

But I wasn't giving up on her. Not after everything she'd been through these past couple of weeks, not to mention the last year. From now on, every problem had to have a solution because there was no way I was letting Mom down.

"I said out of the lake, not out of the water." I let my eyes adjust to the dim light and pulled the drain plug from the rowboat. The wooden seat slipped out of the grooves easily to make room. Once the boat was half full, I plugged the hole to keep the water from draining back out and pulled Mom over the side. "There's no way those Freshie jerks are getting anywhere near you."

Mom lifted her hand out of the water and stroked my cheek.

"Hurricane Jade."

I laughed. "I'm not done yet."

I hooked the rowboat onto the pulley system to lift it out of the water. The chains strained and creaked as they lifted the boat a good four feet out of the water. Good thing Dad had his engineer hat on when he built the boat lift. Ten trips to Home Depot and that thing was strong enough to lift an elephant. And unless those Freshies took lessons from the dolphins at Sea World, there was no way they could get to her.

I poked my head over the side of the boat to see. "You okay in there?"

Mom nodded and smiled.

"What's got you smiling?" It was so nice to see her happy again.

"The thought of the ocean…"

"So, now do you believe I can get you there?"

"If anyone can, it's you…"

I jumped when I heard a car door slam.

"I should go see if that's Gran. You sure you're okay? Is it full enough?"

Mom nodded and sank back into the water in the row-boat. I ducked out the boathouse door and stepped onto the dock.

The sun had disappeared behind the trees, making it hard to see. I glanced up to Gran's cottage, but there were no lights to indicate she was home. Not like I could enlist her in our little plan, but my options were getting very narrow.

Someone giggled. I turned and could just make out

an SUV through the trees. Its running lights dimmed and blinked out. That must have been the car door from before.

Two dark figures strode down toward the Beckers' dock. "Wait for me!"

Chelse.

A deep voice answered. The door of their boathouse creaked open then slammed shut. When I noticed the outline of the canoe still at the dock, a plan started to form. Hopefully, Chelse and her boyfriend would be occupied for a while. I'd need a couple of things from Gran's if this was going to work.

I raced to the cottage and rifled through the junk cupboard in Gran's den. There, I found a mini first-aid kit and the extra fanny pack she used to carry her bingo dabbers.

I dumped out the bandages from the first-aid kit and tested my cell phone in the plastic pouch. Perfect. And waterproof. After my last cell got wrecked, I couldn't take any chances. This phone had already taken a quick dunk back at the Beckers' dock, but now, more than ever, it needed to stay high and dry in case Dad called back.

I popped up to my bedroom in the attic and rifled through my overnight bag. Halfway down the bottom, I found it. The Michaela tankini. It was like a sign.

I stripped off my wet clothes and pulled on the bathing suit along with a dry T-shirt and shorts, then searched my purse for anything else that might come in useful. With the fanny pack snug around my waist, I raced back downstairs and scribbled a note on the back of Gran's Sudoku puzzle book where she was sure to find it.

Hi Gran,
Sleeping over at Cori's. Call me if you need anything. 555-1212.
Love, Jadie
xoxoxo

Finally, I searched the bathroom closet and found the last item on my mental list. I grabbed the container and headed back to the boat shed.

Mom was gonna love this.

Bath salts? Mom's laugh sent a spray of bubbles to the surface of the water. I sprinkled the last of the crystals into the rowboat.

"Not quite the Atlantic Ocean, but I figured you could use a bit of pampering."

It's perfect. She took a deep breath and exhaled it slowly. *Thank you, Jade.*

"It's already dark; we should get going. Ready?"

You sure? Mom asked.

"Surer than sure."

I paddled the canoe until well past midnight, towing the rowboat. The moonlight blazed a path of white light across the rippling waves. The only other light came from the occasional cottages and houses dotting the shores of Talisman Lake.

Right before I'd snatched the canoe from the Becker's wharf, I thought I heard Chelse laugh. I hope she'd forgive me for leaving her stranded, but from the sounds of the deep male voice coming from the boathouse, I didn't think she'd mind an excuse for missing curfew.

I hadn't heard much from the rowboat in the past half hour, and I hoped Mom was resting or at least enjoying the ride. Meanwhile, my hands were beginning to sprout blisters the size of golf balls and something was digging into my right knee.

"How far do you think we've gone?" I hoped I was traveling at least at walking speed but towing a rowboat for five miles, half submerged in water, was proving to be a bit of a handicap.

Instead of Mom's ringing voice I heard splashing from the rowboat.

"What's the matter?" I managed to sidle up with the canoe and checked on her. But the gunwales of the boat were now level with the surface of the lake.

Sinking…

"Darn. The plug must be loose." I untied the bailer. "Can you rest in the lake for a sec?"

Mom moved to the stern, forcing that side of the boat low into the lake. The salt must have given her and extra boost of strength because she slipped easily into the water.

"Can you tell if any Freshies are nearby?" I asked as I bailed.

Mom poked her head out of the water.

"Most of them hang out near the bridge. It's Finalin and Medora we have to worry about. They could be anywhere."

She dove again, then resurfaced.

"I just don't get why the other Freshies just do whatever Finalin tells them to do."

"Finalin and Medora have had a long time to get used to the fresh water and can go as far as Dundee to hunt. They use that little skill as leverage." She disappeared underwater again.

"Hopefully they'll *stay* in Dundee."

Don't worry, I usually hear them before I see them and I'm not hearing anything right now, she called out from below.

"Can they hear us?"

She surfaced. "We should probably keep our conversations above water to be on the safe side. But they wouldn't be able to understand us either way. Mermish and English aren't exactly sister languages."

I shook my head and laughed as I dumped more water back into the lake. "I don't think I'll ever get used to this whole mermaid thing."

Mom dove and swam over to the side of the canoe. Her face emerged from the water.

"You don't ever have to get used to it, Jade. Not if you don't want to." Her eyes held mine and she stroked my hand. "No one will fault you for never wanting to be a part of this life."

It was true. The whole mermaid thing turned my stomach; Mom nailed it. Still, I felt guilty. How could I hate something that was so much a part of me, such a part of Mom? But being a mermaid had only been a big huge pain. And it was the thing keeping Mom from being home with us, where she belonged.

I changed the subject.

"You sound much better." I bailed the water as quickly as I could until the rowboat sat higher in the water, then made sure the plug was snug.

"The salt really helped."

"Some probably leaked out along the way, but there should still be a little left. You should get back in before anyone notices you."

Mom slipped back over the stern and settled in.

"Is that okay?" I asked.

Mom nodded, just below the surface.

I started paddling again, digging deep into the water to get the momentum of the canoe and rowboat going.

I wish there was something I could do to help, Mom called from within the rowboat.

"Believe me, once you get back home, you are SO baking me cookies," I joked.

My hands ached as the paddle's wooden shaft rubbed at my blistered palms. I tried to distract myself and thought back to when I'd gotten my first period. How I'd wished Mom was there to ask questions. So much had changed in just a few short weeks. I'd turned into a mermaid (twice), escaped from a horde of criminal mer-people, and rescued Mom from a makeshift dock prison.

Ha! If I could get through all that, a few blisters weren't about to hold me back.

I paddled for another hour or so, when suddenly, off in the distance, a string of lights caught my eye.

"It's the bridge!"

I heard Mom lift her head out of the water, no doubt turning to see. "You did it, Jade!"

"I know!" I couldn't remember a time when I felt so happy. I paddled and focused on the bridge lights, imagining what it would be like when Mom was home. Finally home.

Then, as I pulled the paddle back, I felt something brush my hand.

Something damp and hairy.

I screamed.

"What? What is it?" Mom asked.

They found us.

"The Freshies!"

I brought my canoe paddle up and whacked at the hands with the blade. They grabbed at the sides of the boat between blows.

"Jade!" Mom's pale face shone like the moon in the dim light.

"They must have followed the salt water from the leaky plug."

Whack! Whack!

"Be careful!" Mom called out.

The canoe shifted and juddered beneath me as I struck

the hands with the paddle. But there was another motion. A rocking motion. I reached out to steady myself.

"They're trying to tip me over!" I called out to Mom, but I'm sure that by the time my words reached her ears, I was already in the water.

And sinking fast.

Chapter Sixteen

T HE LAKE SWALLOWED ME whole, shutting me off from the night air. It licked its cool, watery tongue along my arms and legs and pricked my skull with its icy claws. Hands locked around my arms and legs, forcing me down.

My hair swirled wildly around my face as I flailed in the water, trying to get away. A familiar panic overwhelmed me as water shot through to my lungs, driving the air from my nose and mouth.

Breathe! Just breathe! I forced myself to inhale, disgusted by the gurgling sensation as water flooded my lungs but relieved that I didn't gag. The panic fell away and something deep inside of me took over. It came from the horror of seeing Mom disappear underwater that day last summer, the countless nights crying myself to sleep, the look of helplessness in Dad's eyes.

These monsters had caused it all.

Every last bit.

Get off me! I rang out the words into the dark depths of

the lake and tried to kick the Freshies away. They let go of my ankles, only to grasp their hands along my legs to get hold of my wrists. I struggled to break free, but could only writhe and twist in their clutches as they wrenched my arms behind my back. *You bottom-dwelling, scum-sucking jerks!*

The Freshies' foreign voices rang all around me. One wrapped its arm around my throat. I kicked at them but could already feel my legs begin to fuse. How much longer before it was too late and I became one of them?

A rush of warm water shot down from above. I turned my face upward. The moon shone behind Mom, casting a perfect silhouette, as she dumped the rowboat to its side and dove into the water toward me. She let out an ear-piercing screech. The Freshies loosened their grips in surprise.

I turned and bit down hard.

Aieeeeeaaaa!

I shrugged from their grasp and swam to Mom with the mer-dudes at what were still my feet. But as I swam, the salt water from the rowboat passed over my body.

Oh, yeah. That thing Mom said about salt water boosting the mermaid transformation?

Understatement.

My legs exploded into a tail, this time, ripping my shorts and the tankini bottom from my body. Mom and the Freshies fell back from the force of the transformation. The fabric floated away in shreds.

That was an eighty dollar bathing suit, you morons! I yelled over my shoulder as rage overtook me—not about the suit, but from being forced underwater like that. Being pulled down with hateful hands and made a mermaid. Not given the choice.

It set my whole body on fire.

My new mermaid body felt clumsy, like swimming with my legs tied together, but my vision and hearing cleared, sharpening the sights and sounds around me. I searched the water for Mom and realized she had taken my place, fighting off Finalin and Medora.

They had her!

Get away from her! I dove toward them, not quite knowing how to move my tail, grabbing the water and pushing it away to make it down to Mom.

Swim, Jade! Get out of here! Mom rang.

But I wasn't going anywhere. I felt for the fanny pack, still attached to my waist.

Finalin turned to me and sneered. He nodded to Medora and rang out an obnoxious series of rings. I didn't need to speak Mermish to know he was mocking me. And that ticked me off even more.

I said—get your hairy, stinking hands off my mother!

Maybe it was the way I said it, or the tone of my voice, but Finalin and Medora looked like they got the gist because they stopped and looked from me to Mom. Finalin seemed to do the whole mental math a lot quicker than Medora because soon, his voice whirred at a speed that made my ears hurt.

Mom responded with a string of rings of her own.

While Finalin continued ranting, I reached into my

fanny pack and pulled out the pepper spray I'd grabbed from my purse back at Gran's cottage.

Look away, I yelled to Mom.

I turned my face and sprayed.

At first, there was nothing. But then, the pepper spray must have drifted into Finalin and Medora's faces because soon, the whole underwater realm filled with a deafening ring.

I caught Mom's hand.

Swim! I yelled.

I whipped the tail like I'd seen the dolphins do on our last trip to Sea World and amazed myself with the fact that I was actually keeping up with Mom. We swam with all our might, leaving the Freshies in our wake. My hair skimmed my shoulders as the water slipped past.

Wow.

You're getting the hang of this, Mom rang out.

But I didn't want to get the hang of it. I wanted to get out of there, out of the water, out of that nightmare. *Can you tell if they're following us?* I kept my eyes straight ahead, not daring to look.

Whatever you did seems to be keeping them occupied. I have a feeling they'll be back though. What was that stuff, anyway?

Pepper spray. Having an overprotective dad comes in handy sometimes. Could Finalin understand what I was saying?

I just filled in the blanks a bit. We swam to the edge of the lake and found the creek. *Let's hide in here,* Mom said.

I followed her in. *Won't this be the first place they look?*

Mom laughed. *Those two are mean as dirt, but they're not the sharpest narwhals in the pod.*

I laughed a humongous snort bubble. *I think I've just been introduced to my first taste of mermish humor.*

We grabbed some sticks and branches and piled them at the mouth of the creek. But the water in the creek had the same thin feeling as it did weeks before. Only, after sprinting to get there and building the dam so quickly, I struggled more than ever to catch my breath.

What's the matter? Mom asked.

I can't stay in here. I swam to the edge of the creek and began to haul myself out.

I coughed and sputtered as my head shot out of the water. My lungs sucked in a gulp full of air like a helium balloon being filled at the party store. I stayed, half in, half out of the creek and worked to steady my breathing. A short while later, my tail began to burn, heating up the water all around it and soon, steam rose from the surface.

Are you okay? Mom swam toward me and brushed my tail.

"I think so," I said breathlessly. "No…" I hurled lake water and my semi-digested Hungry Man entrée and Chocolate Mug Cake onto the creek's bank.

"Oh, Jade." Mom emerged from the water for a moment and pulled my hair away from my face.

"Sorry…I've got to figure out how to stop puking like that." I fell back against a rock and closed my eyes.

"You get that from your dad." Mom grinned.

I laughed, remembering all the amusement park rides Mom would take me on while Dad held the cotton candy. The cool water from the stream took the edge off the searing pain. It was only about half as bad as the last time. "I'll be… okay." I struggled to keep my breath steady.

"Incredible." Mom held my hand and stroked my tail as it transformed into legs. Meanwhile, millions of shards of pain ran up and down my skin. "It took weeks for me to do this in the tidal pool…"

When it was over, I pulled myself out of the water and collapsed onto the bank.

Mom's face rose through the water once more. "I can't believe how quickly you can change back and forth."

"What can I say? I'm an overachiever." My lower half was bare. "I'm also half naked. How can you stand that?"

"Occupational hazard."

I pulled my shirt off, leaving the top of the tankini, and wrapped the shirt around my middle.

"Oh no, I left the fanny pack open when I pepper sprayed Finalin and Medora."

I fumbled inside, relieved that everything was still there, and pulled out my cell phone from the waterproof first aid container.

"A message!"

It was from Dad. I put it on speakerphone for Mom to hear.

"Jade, I just got your message! There's a return flight leaving from Dallas in about 20 minutes. I'm just waiting to see if I can get on. It's 5:20 a.m. your time which should put me back in Port Toulouse around 11 if there are no delays. Tell Mom I love her…and you too…"

I rushed to call back but was too late. "He must be on the plane again."

Mom blinked and nodded then disappeared underwater.

I stood and stretched my legs. Port Toulouse stood still in the early morning light. A lone car crossed the bridge. Thankfully, we were well hidden behind the low alders skirting the creek and the stand of whispering aspens. I couldn't see the ocean past the bridge from where I stood but could imagine the sun rising over the horizon.

"Once Dad's here, we'll get you to the ocean. Otherwise, we'll figure out how to escape when the Martins' sailboat goes through the lock. One way or another, a few more hours and you'll be free."

Mom sat upright in the creek. Water ran off her dark hair in rivulets.

"They're coming."

I heard it. The high-pitched whine of Finalin accompanied by the screeching whirr of Medora. To anyone else, it may have sounded like the buzzing of electrical wires or spring cicadas. To me though, the sounds were like nails on a chalkboard.

I ran to the edge of the lake, looking for the telltale signs of lurking mer-dudes. I thought I saw a flicker a couple of hundred feet away. The rowboat had drifted against the nearby rock shield, giving me an idea. I pulled it to the mouth of the creek and jammed it in, along with the branches we'd assembled.

"What are you doing?" Mom asked.

"Just adding a bit of reinforcement."

Once I finished barricading the creek with extra branches, logs, and any rock I could find (there weren't many left after the mer-blockade), I took the rowboat's bowline and tied it tightly around one of the aspens on shore.

"Here they come."

Finalin and Medora did their best to break through our dam, but with an unfortunate lack of legs, plus the fact I kept whacking them with a canoe paddle from the safety of the creek's bank, they were at a bit of a disadvantage.

Finally, after an hour of trying, they gave up. I collapsed on the bank once Mom signaled they were gone.

They usually hide out during the day. Rest for a bit. I'll let you know if I hear them come back. Mom stayed underwater as she rang out the words, seeming to lack the strength to even lift her head out of the water. The creek's thin, fresh water was making her weaker. Only, after having spent weeks imprisoned in Dundee, it seemed to catch up with her even quicker.

"Are you sure you'll be okay?" I stifled a yawn.

Neither of us will be getting out of here unless you get some rest.

It didn't take much convincing. I curled up on the bank of the creek and drifted into a coma-like sleep.

My cell woke me up, seconds later.

"Dad?!" I screamed.

"No, Jade. It's me. I'm at Mug Glug's."

Cori.

The water in the creek had collected into a deep pool behind the dam. Mom's eyes were closed but her chest rose and fell in shallow breaths below surface. I checked my watch. How could it be past eleven already? Had I really passed out for the last six hours?

"Cori." I tried to figure out a story that would fit. One that wouldn't tip off what a pathetic loser I was for inviting her to Mug Glug's and never showing up.

"You weren't in school. Aren't you coming?" she asked.

Ugh. I hated this.

"I'm so sorry," I continued. "I stayed up way too late last night…"

The truth.

"And slept in."

The truth.

"There's no way I could make it there on time."

A lie. I could see Mug Glug's awning reflected in the barbershop's windows from where I sat.

"I'm not even dressed."

Kinda true, since a tankini top, a fanny pack, and a T-shirt stretched across my behind didn't really qualify as dressed.

There was silence on the other end of the line. I glanced up to the barbershop window. Cori's reflection stood on the street outside of Mug Glug's now, giving up on our hot chocolate date. It killed me to have to mislead her like that.

Would Lainey do the same? I doubted it. Though Lainey's mom owned a fashion studio and mine was an aquatic mammal. Not exactly the same level of complication.

"Well, why don't we just meet at the lock for the boat cruise?" Cori asked. I could see her, shrugging her shoulders with the question, her chin hunched down into her chest as she talked into her cell. She was trying, *really* trying, and all I could do was scramble for a new lie to fend her off. "Trey said Luke got a text from you. You're still coming, aren't you?"

This got harder and harder.

I gazed at the boat lock, the only thing between Mom and me and the ocean. Once Dad got there or the Martins' sailboat went through and gave us the chance to escape, this would all be over. Then, maybe I could get back on track with Cori.

But what if the Freshies didn't let us through, and even then, what if the sentries stopped us at the end of the canal? I shook my head. Would life ever be normal again?

"I'm sorry, Cori. I've just got a lot going on right now. It's just not really a great time." Talk about understatement of the century.

"What's going on, Jade? Maybe I can help."

If only she could, but our only hope lay with Dad, who was probably on his way to Port Toulouse by now. What if he was trying to call?

"Listen, I'm sorry. I really gotta go."

Talk about being a bottom-dwelling, scum-sucking jerk.

"I'm sorry too." But her sorry sounded like something different. Not an apology, but more of a regret.

She hung up before I could say good-bye.

Chapter Seventeen

I DIALED DAD'S NUMBER AS soon as I hung up with Cori.

I could see Mom's eyelids flutter through the water. She lay limp, like when I'd found her under the dock. I needed to get her out of the creek and into salt water again. A big, wide ocean would have come in handy right about then.

Dad picked up on the first ring.

"Sorry, honey, I'm driving as fast as I can but I'm still an hour away. How's Mom?"

"She's holding on, but I'm not sure for how long." I moved to the creek's opening and crouched behind a bush to look across the lake. The Martins' sailboat cruised toward the bridge. I could see Luke and Trey sitting above deck.

Shoot! They were early.

"The Martins are about to go through the lock with their sailboat. I was thinking I'd help Mom swim across, but maybe we should wait for you instead."

Getting Mom through the boat lock meant becoming a mermaid again. Every other time, the change had been kind of forced on me. This time, *I'd* be the one making the choice. I wasn't sure I could do it.

"Do you think she could make it if we carried her over the bridge to the other side of the lock?" Dad asked.

I turned back to see Mom. Her eyes were closed again. Dundee had zapped more out of her than I imagined. If she couldn't stay strong in the creek, how could she survive out of the water long enough for us to transport her to the ocean?

"I don't think so. Especially not if we have to wait until after dark."

Luke and Trey were standing now, preparing the bow and stern lines. The lights were already flashing on the bridge's barriers, signaling for the cars to stop. I heard a long car horn sound through the cell phone and could imagine Dad trying to drive and talk. Definitely a safety issue, given his engineer's predisposition for non-lateral thinking.

"Dad, hang up the phone and just get here when you can."

"What are you going to do?" he asked.

"I'm not exactly sure," I answered.

"Stay safe."

"You too," I said before disconnecting. I made a quick call to Gran to let her know I'd made it to school (not!) and tucked the cell back into my fanny pack, safe inside the waterproof container. The sailboat made steady progress across the lake. If we wanted to follow the boat through the lock, we'd need to move fast. Someone else must have had the same thing in mind though, judging by the telltale flicks following the boat and the annoying chatter ringing in my ears.

"Ugly and Uglier are back," I called back to Mom.

The others can't be far behind. Mom's chest heaved as she spoke.

Soon, two paths turned into over a dozen. To anyone else, it may have looked like a school of trout, or water striders flicking across the water. But to me, all I saw was competition.

"You mean we're going to have to fight through the crowds to get to the lock?" I asked.

Like Hyde's during after-Christmas sales, Mom joked.

"And they're all trying to escape?"

A fizz of bubbles escaped from Mom's mouth as she laughed. *Not escape. No one ever escapes...just trying to keep me in.*

I understood. If Mom got to talk to the sentries, the Mermish Council would know what happened and would probably let her through. Then, the Freshies' chance to become human would be lost forever.

"How many are we talking?" I asked.

Last count...about fourteen of us.

"Don't say 'us'!" Bitter bile rose to my throat. "Don't lump yourself in with the rest of those freaks."

Mom gathered her energy and swam over to our rowboat dam.

Medora and Finalin aside, some of those mers have become my friends.

I ignored that last part. How could Mom even think of considering any of those jerks her friends?

"What if they won't let us through?"

Jade, sweetie. You don't need to do this, Mom said. *We can wait for your dad.*

Looking at Mom, so weak and tired, I tried to decide what to do. I could see Cori and Lainey waiting for the Martins on the concrete pier next to the boat lock. Shaky Eddie was back in his control tower after weeks away. The sailboat got closer and closer.

I felt like a damsel in distress on one of those old Saturday morning cartoons, tied up on a railroad track with a train screaming toward me. If there was ever a time when I could use a dashing young hero, this would be it. But it was up to me. I had to decide.

Would I dive in the lake and force myself underwater? Become one of *them* again? I imagined the panicky feeling of water flooding my lungs, the alien tail taking over my lower body…could I do something I hated *so* much if it meant saving Mom?

No contest.

I ran to untie the rowboat from the trunk of the aspen, then splashed into the creek beside Mom. "We didn't come this far to give up now. You ready?" I braced my hands against the rowboat, ready to push it out of the way.

Mom pulled her hair back from her face as she surfaced.

"Are you sure?" Her voice was barely a whisper.

"Sure as I've ever been."

"I feel sorry for anyone who tries to stop you," Mom said with a smile. She slipped back underwater. *Nice bathing suit by the way.*

"Perfect for kicking some mer-dude butt."

I shoved the rowboat out of the way and plunged into the lake, pulling Mom's limp body onto my back as I dove. Water burned my throat as it flooded into my lungs. I struggled to steady my breath, resisting the urge to gag and escape back to the surface of the lake. But I couldn't. Not with the Martins' boat cruising down the lake toward the lock. Someone was bound to see. I kept whipping my legs, pushing the water away with my free hand and hanging on to Mom with the other. My thighs had already begun to fuse but the salt water closer to the lock ramped up the transformation, exploding my legs into a mermaid's tail.

Like a fish to water.

Sorry about the bumpy ride, I rang back to Mom. Her laugh made me smile. And even though the tail felt gross and wrong on my body, I hoped I'd made the right choice.

It only took a few minutes to get to the base of the bridge. Mom was right. The Freshies crowded at the lock like kids at the exit doors on the last day of school. They pushed and shoved, waiting by the massive metal gate. How the heck were we supposed to get through? Some of them were big. Really big. One looked like she was around my age though. She caught me staring and looked away.

Juvenile delinquent? I asked.

Mom slid off my back. The salt seemed to give her a bit more energy, but still, her whole body drooped with exhaustion.

She's Medora and Finalin's daughter, Mom said quietly. *Her name's Serena.*

Does a life of crime run in the family or something?

No, she was born here... Mom said quietly... *in captivity.*

You mean she's never seen the ocean? Something about that brought a lump to my throat, but I didn't have time to dwell on the Mermish Young Offenders Act because just then, Finalin and Medora pushed their way through the pod.

Just remember, Mom reminded me, *those guys have two things on their minds: escaping to the ocean or becoming human.*

And they figure we have the answer to at least one of those, I added.

Pretty much.

I held up the pepper spray. *Gave up on your rock piling career, huh?* I rang as they approached.

Finalin and Medora cowered at the sight of the can. They screeched something at Mom.

What are they saying?

They've come to make a deal, Mom said.

Tell them to go suck frogs.

Let's just listen to what they have to say.

Impressively, Finalin held back the other Freshies with just a wave of his hand. He'd obviously been holding food and the promise of foot-dom over their heads for a while, judging by the way the rest of the Freshies followed his commands like pathetic sheep. Medora spoke to Mom in hushed rings. I understood right away.

They wanted to tag along and rush the sentries.

No way!

The nerve! The absolute freaking nerve of them!

I could see the hull of the Martin's sailboat approaching. Dad was nowhere in sight. I pulled Mom aside. It was now or never and we didn't have time for this.

They think now that I have this pepper spray we're their ticket to freedom? Well they can forget it.

Mom drew my flowing hair away from my face. *Honey, think about it: Finalin just has to wave his hand and that can is history. We need to be smart about this. There are way more of them than us.*

Medora and Finalin's daughter floated behind them. Her eyes were red, like she'd been crying. Her parents pulled her close and looked to us for an answer. It's then that I realized they weren't just trying to escape from the lake prison for themselves, they were doing it for her. I could see it in their eyes. That's why they'd acted so strangely when they figured out I was Mom's daughter.

Finalin and Medora deserved to rot in this muddy, pond scum lake. Serena, on the other hand, didn't ask for any of this, just like I didn't ask to have Mom taken away from me.

We'll take her. I pointed and whispered to Mom. *Only her.*

Mom turned to me.

Are you sure? What if they don't agree?

The warning signal continued to clang through the water as the bridge's deck lifted upward. The large metal gate of the lock groaned open.

They'd better. Have them call off the others so we can talk.

Finalin and Medora should have traded in their life of crime for a career in contract negotiations because after a couple of minutes of squeaks and trills, the other Freshies dispersed just as the hull of the Martins' sailboat passed above us.

We have three minutes, tops. Tell them we'll take her through, but alone, and once she's there, she's on her own. That's the deal.

There was an exchange of rings and tones. At first, I didn't think they'd go for it. After all they'd put Mom through in the past year, trying to escape, I couldn't imagine them giving up without a fight. One way or another, we had to move fast. The Martins' boat was already inside the lock. Soon, the gate would close and we'd all be stranded. Again.

Then a miracle happened.

Medora and Finalin hugged their daughter.

And swam away.

We made it safely into the lock just as the gate screeched to a close. It would take a while longer before the water in the lock rose to meet the level of the ocean so Eddie could open the second gate. Mom and I waited under the Martins' stern. Serena huddled at the bow.

She's scared, Mom whispered.

No doubt terrified by stories of the pepper-spray-wielding half-human mer-girl. Mom tried to encourage her to join us with soothing tones, but Serena didn't budge.

I can't believe I felt sorry her. I sighed.

That's because you're a good person, Jade. Mom stroked my hair.

I don't feel like much of a good person these days. I thought of how I'd ditched Cori at the coffee shop and how I'd told Luke I would come on the boat cruise, then didn't show up for either. I had a lot of things to make up for.

And yes, I felt bad for Serena, but my sympathy only went so far. She was the spawn of *those jerks* after all. The ones who'd stolen Mom from me for almost a year.

But that would all change if we could just get past the sentries.

Mom swam over to the sluice where the ocean water poured in. She closed her eyes and let the current of the water flow over her. Maybe it was the salt or just the promise of what was just beyond the wall, but her energy was definitely back.

I looked up through the water, trying to figure out how long we'd have to wait. Luke and Trey tied up the sailboat along the canal wall and greeted Cori and Lainey on the concrete pier edging the canal. The girls' forms shimmered through the water as they boarded. Lainey stretched out her hand for Luke to help her board, then she disappeared onto the boat, away from view.

Luke hung back on the dock, glancing down into the water. I slipped under the boat and peeked out from behind the hull. Had something fallen in? Hopefully one of Lainey's very expensive earrings. Okay. That wasn't very nice. It wasn't her fault I wasn't up there, enjoying a boat cruise on a hot summer day. And she might as well take my place since there was no way Luke would give me the time of day now. Not after texting him to re-invite myself and then never showing up.

Luke climbed up the control tower to talk to his grandfather. Probably to ask him to keep an eye out for whatever had fallen. After a few minutes, Trey hopped out of the boat to help him untie the lines. I turned to look for Mom when I heard the second metal gate screech open.

Mom, it's time.

Serena and I joined her at the gate. She took us each by the arm.

We still have a bit of a swim before we get to the end of the canal. That's where the sentries will be waiting. They may buy my story, but who knows if they'll let you guys through. Mom held out her hand. *Better give me the pepper spray just in case.*

No, I'll take care of the sentries and you guys make a break for it. I pulled the canister from my fanny pack and shut the zipper. Serena cowered.

Jade, those guys don't mess around. I'd feel better if you gave me the pepper spray.

The gate opened wider. The sound from the sailboat's revving engine reverberated in the lock as the Martins set off, dragging their stern line. A rush of water from the propeller pushed us backward. My palm slipped from Mom's hand.

Swim, honey! Mom called out. But the force of the water was too great for my brand new mermaid body and I fell back.

I can't.

Eddie climbed down from his tower and followed the boat along the canal's pier. He cupped his hands around his mouth. What was he saying? Was he telling them about the stern line dragging behind the boat? I hoped not.

Get the line! I pointed.

Serena and Mom grabbed the stern line and Mom reached back for me. *Take my hand!*

I'm right behind you. Just hold on! I trailed behind them, pepper spray in hand, and swam with all my might, following the sailboat as it cruised down the canal to the ocean. But by the time I caught up with them, the sentries weren't there!

Where are they? I asked, finally grabbing the rope.

Look! Mom pointed through the crystal blue waters of Port Toulouse Bay. Shaky Eddie had fallen in the waters of the bay! His lily white legs thrashed in the water. I watched in horror as the sentries grabbed Eddie and pulled him away.

What are they doing to him?! I stole glances over my shoulder as we sailed away.

Lucky for us, it looks like they're rescuing him! Mom grasped my hand.

Chapter Eighteen

SERENA DIDN'T LAST LONG. Maybe it was the constant threat of the pepper spray canister in my hand, but she'd let go of the stern line and disappeared through a forest of kelp not long after we reached the ocean.

Mom and I had hidden behind the hull while the Martins turned the boat around to pick up Eddie. I caught a glimpse of him wrapped up in blankets on the upper deck.

We hung on until the Martins' sailboat reached the D'Escousse marina. Mom was already looking much better, new and improved by the salty ocean water. I was just happy to be far, far away from the sludgy lake and scary mer-dudes.

Do you think Eddie is okay? I asked.

He should be fine. The sentries got to him pretty fast. Mermish Code of Ethics, Council Decree 419. We're always supposed to come to the aid of humans in trouble.

How did he fall in the water in the first place?

Maybe he had a little extra something in his coffee this morning, Mom joked.

We both laughed, sending a fizz of bubbles up to the surface of the water. I watched them rise, mesmerized by my new reality.

A mer-girl.

I would have never believed that I could be so happy like this, in the water with Mom. It all seemed like a dream.

What about Serena? Even though she was the daughter of two of the most disgusting creatures on the planet, I couldn't help but feel sorry for her. She'd not only lost her mom but her dad too, but also, now she was in the big wide ocean, away from the life she'd always known in the lake.

I'll go find her a little later on. Don't worry. Mom smiled.

Through the shimmering surface of the water, I could see Mr. and Mrs. Martin hop out onto the dock to greet another man and a woman holding a toddler. Luke and Trey followed behind them. The little boy struggled down from his mother's arms and ran to Luke.

"Stewie! Hey, there buddy!" Luke's voice sounded through the water as he twirled the boy in the air.

Stewie? Was this their cousin, Stewart, they'd talked about back at the sports field that day?

Huh.

Cori and Lainey chatted up on the boat's deck. I strained to hear but couldn't make out what they were saying. Not surprising since I was a whole hull away from my usual normal teenaged life.

Where exactly *did* I belong? Was it there in the water with Mom, swimming the ocean blue? Or with a bunch of friends, celebrating the last day of school? Did I even *have* friends after all that had happened in the past few weeks?

You look like you're a million miles away, Mom said.

Huh? Oh. I was just thinking about how weird this all was.

It's a lot to take in. The skin of Mom's cheeks glowed with a pink blush as she smiled, just like I remembered. *But at least you're open to a whole new dietary selection.* She plucked barnacles off the jetty and sucked them, hungrily. *Mm, I'd forgotten what good seafood tasted like.*

That's disgusting! I cringed.

Mom laughed.

What did you think mers ate?

Oh, I don't know. Maybe something slightly less revolting? I wrinkled my nose. *I have a feeling I wouldn't have much trouble managing my weight living here with you.*

Well, you shouldn't even be thinking like that. Mom took my hand and led me through the vertical poles of the jetty.

Where are we going? I swam behind her, flicking my tail to keep up.

We need to get you out of the water. We reached an out-cropping of large boulders underneath a darkened area of the pier.

Wait. No. I'm not going anywhere yet. But Mom couldn't hear me over the sound of the surf crashing against the rocks.

The boathouse is right over us. No one will see you call Dad from here, she continued.

Mom! I flicked my tail toward her and tugged at her hand. A school of minnows shot off in the opposite direction as the word pierced the water.

Mom turned. *What's the matter? Do you still have the phone?*

Yes, but I don't want to go until you're ready to come home too. We still have to find the tidal pool...

Aw, Jade. Water rushed around me as Mom drew me into her arms. *Come here, sweetie.*

Let me come with you. My whole body shuddered. But from the way Mom stroked my face, I could tell the answer was no.

You can't stay here. Mom's hair danced around her face in flowing, dark swirls.

She wrapped her hands around my waist and lifted me out of the water onto one of the rocks. Streams of water ran down my body and along my tail, then back into the ocean. I gagged as water forced its way out of my lungs and I tried my best to suck in breaths of air between coughs.

Mom's face emerged from the water. She smiled.

"You belong on land with Dad. And up there with your friends."

I glanced through the slats of the jetty's deck and could see Cori, Trey, Lainey, and Luke a dozen or so feet away. Did I really belong there with them, chatting about summer plans? I didn't feel like I belonged anywhere just then.

"Call Dad before it happens." She nodded to my tail, which was already getting hot.

The thought of Dad brought me back to reality. He was probably back in Port Toulouse by now, worried sick and wondering if we were okay. What would it do to him, not knowing if we were all right? I pulled the cell from the waterproof pouch in my waist pack. A fine mist had collected inside the screen.

"I don't think cell phones were meant for deep sea diving." Thankfully, the key pad lit up as I dialed the number.

He picked up on the first ring.

"Jade!" His voice rang through the earpiece. "Where are you? How's Micci?"

"Mom's fine. She's right here."

Mom shook her head. She didn't want to talk to him. I tried to avoid his next question.

"I'm at the D'Escousse marina, under the dock by the boat house. Can you come get me?" I winced as the scales on my tail began to burn.

"Stay there. I'm pulling out of Bridget's parking lot right now."

Beep-beeep! A car horn sounded in the background.

"Dad!" I yelled over the sound of the crashing waves, then lowered my voice. "Dad…"

"Yes?" Dad's voice came out as a gasp over the phone.

"Hang up the phone and drive," I said.

"Good point." I could hear the smile in Dad's voice as he hung up.

I snapped the phone shut and shifted on the hard rock, trying to block the hot pain as it worked its way through my tail.

"Is it bad?" Mom's face emerged from the water, her

forehead wrinkled with worry. She stroked my tail with a wet hand.

"It helps when you do that." I winced and welcomed her hand along the scales. It felt like running cool water on a burned finger, but each time her hand left my tail so she could dive to catch her breath underwater, a million new needle pricks pierced my flesh.

My whole body screamed as the scales reabsorbed, one by one, into my skin. Soon though, the tail transformed and I was changed back to my alter ego: two-legged Jade.

"Hey, I didn't puke!" I said in surprise.

"Your dad would be so proud," Mom replied with a smile.

"Why didn't you want to talk to him?" I asked quietly.

Mom blinked and turned away. I reached down for her hand and pulled her up.

"Mom. Tell me."

She looked up through the slats of the dock.

"You see those people up there?" She whispered over the sound of the waves around us. I watched as people walked along the pier above us, oblivious of the one and a half mermaids below, just a few meters away. "Dad knows me as a human. Like that."

She slipped back underwater.

"But don't you want to see him?"

The tones of Mom's voice were low and twinkled in my ear. *Of course I do. Just not like this.*

Just then, I could hear Cori and Lainey's voices as two sets of feet clicked to a stop overhead.

Is that our little Cori? Mom whispered in a low ring.

And my evil nemesis, I rang back.

I shrunk back against one of the vertical poles, well hidden by the darkened space. I could make out Cori's lean brown legs and Lainey's wedged heels (totally inappropriate for boating, I might add) through the cracks between the boards of the dock.

"I *cannot* believe that guy," Lainey whined. "He asks me to come on this stupid boat cruise and all he can do is text Scissor Lips. What does he see in her, anyway?"

I winced at the nickname. Almost three years later, it still stung. I flipped open my phone. I hadn't yet noticed the three text messages that flashed back.

New messages received from fluke1019

10:45   u coming?

11:17   leaving in 10

1:23   u ok?

Me. He was texting me.

"Scissor Lips?" Cori replied. "That's just mean. Why would you call her that?"

"Well I *gave* her the nickname. I figure I'm entitled to use it." Lainey's laugh carried through the dock's decking and reverberated around me.

My fists clenched at my sides. *Lainey? She* was the one who'd made junior high hell for me with that nickname?! All this time, I'd blamed Luke. But it wasn't him. It was never him.

I felt like stomping up to the dock and carrying out my eyelash plucking fantasy, but given the fact that I was dressed in only a tankini top with a T-shirt wrapped around my waist, I figured I'd stay put.

"Well, first of all," Cori replied, "her name is *Jade*. And second, you kind of invited yourself on this boat cruise."

"How was I supposed to know Stewart was a whiny, grubby-nosed ankle biter? I thought Luke was setting her up! And anyway, he should be with someone like me, not her."

I replayed all of my recent conversations with Luke in my head. He wasn't mocking me about my braces when I ran over him at Dooley's, he was being *nice*. He didn't invite me on the boat cruise to set me up on a pity date; he was being a good friend!

"You know what, Lainey?" Cori said. "Maybe *you* should be the one hanging out with Stewart. You seem to have a lot in common."

"Well, if that's how you feel, maybe I should ask Mother to reconsider your co-op mentorship."

"Fine."

"Well, fine!"

Both sets of feet clicked away toward the boat.

"That's my Cori," I whispered to Mom.

Can I assume this had something to do with a boy? Mom asked.

"Maybe." I smiled.

Mom turned toward the ocean then pulled herself partway out of the water and hugged my legs. "I should go." She gave my knee a kiss and slipped back into the water. "I love you."

"Do you really have to go now?" Everything was happening so fast. Too fast.

Mom nodded as she hovered underwater. Her hair floated to the surface and mixed with the strands of seaweed waving back and forth in the surf.

Leave me the phone.

"But the battery's almost gone." My eyes blurred as I turned the power off on the phone.

Don't worry. I'll use my other shell phone to make overseas calls. Mom smirked.

I snorted.

"You only have two bars left. Just turn it back on when you need it." I tucked the phone back in the waterproof pack and wedged it between two rocks beside me. "Can you get it from there?"

"Yes." Mom smiled and blew me a kiss. She dove through the crystal waters of the ocean, her long ebony hair flowing behind her.

Then, she was gone.

By the time Dad picked me up, the Martins' sailboat had just left the dock.

He was crying when he found me. Big fat tears, his face red and puffy.

"She's gone, Dad." It killed me to tell him what Mom had said. How she only wanted to see him when she was human again. Dad stared off into the ocean as I tried to explain, but even with his body turned, I could imagine the world of hurt all over his face.

He turned to help me up.

"Are you okay? Here, put this on." Dad pulled off his buttoned down shirt and wrapped it around me. We walked back to the parking lot—Dad in his undershirt, me barefoot—and ducked into the car before attracting too much attention.

I told Dad the whole story, from when I found Mom at the Beckers' dock, to the Freshies, the sentries, and how Shaky Eddie had fallen in the water. For some reason, that made Dad laugh.

"What's so funny?" I yawned as we pulled onto the highway.

"I'm just glad everyone's okay." Dad patted my hand. "You should rest. We can talk more later."

We drove along the route from D'Escousse to Port Toulouse, catching peeks of the ocean as the sun blazed pink and orange streaks across the horizon. Exhaustion set in as we wound our way along the road and my head began to nod in that open-mouth head-bob that's so attractive.

Dad turned on the local radio station to fill the dead air. The news came on after a medley of honky-tonk songs:

"A man from Port Toulouse narrowly escaped drowning this afternoon. 'I thought I was a goner,' Edward Schroemenger said in a telephone interview. 'But the current must have been with me because it brought me right to shore.' A reminder for everyone to practice water safety as the summer gets into full swing."

I snapped awake. "Schroemenger? I thought Eddie's last name was Martin, like Luke's."

Dad smiled. "Eddie is Luke's grandfather on his mom's side."

I tried to line up the facts in my head.

"So, Eddie Schroemenger—as in, Dr. E. Schroemenger? The mer expert?"

Dad's face broke into a goofy grin.

"I was going to tell you tomorrow after you'd gotten some rest. I heard the radio report on my way to pick you up, so I looked it up."

"Don't tell me you were under the influence of Google while operating a motor vehicle."

"This was a special case." Dad winked. "Apparently, Eddie spent summers around here for many years while he was a professor. Probably because of its high mer concentration. Once the university revoked his tenure after that article came out, he decided to move up here permanently."

"So, he probably knows all about the mers in Talisman Lake. It *must* have been him who pulled the hoodie over me that day I passed out next to the creek. And he must have seen us in the canal and figured out what we were doing." It's then that I realized, he didn't fall; he jumped!

"I'm sure Eddie has seen it all in his day, especially working at the boat lock. Once things settle down, maybe we can pay him a bit of a visit."

Would Eddie know how long it would take for Mom to become human again so she could come home? I wondered.

We drove in silence for a while longer. Dad concentrated on the road ahead as his yellow fog lights swept back and forth with every bend in the road.

His phone rang.

"I can get it." I reached my hand out for the phone.

"Probably just work. I told John I'd call him once I got back in town." He pulled the phone from his pocket and flipped it open. "John…"

But it wasn't John. From the way Dad's whole body straightened and he drew in a sharp breath, it could only be one person.

"Micci. How…"

…was she able to call him?

"Why…"

…wouldn't she see him?

"Where…"

…was she right now?

"Really?" Dad's voice rose to an excited pitch. "How long will that take? How will I know when to come get you?"

"Will the Council show her where the tidal pool is?" I asked.

He turned and nodded, sporting the biggest grin I'd seen in a long while.

The fog lights danced across the yellow line, onto the oncoming car, against the guardrail.

"Dad. Dad!"

He glanced my way.

"What?"

I braced my hand against the dashboard and pointed to the side of the road.

"Just a second, Micci, don't go anywhere."

Dad tucked the phone between his ear and his shoulder and braced his hands on the steering wheel to guide the car to the side of the road. He put the car in park.

"Sorry about that..." His voice went quiet as he brought his hands to the phone and tucked his chin to his chest. "Our daughter is in the car with me. I thought it would be a good idea to pull over to keep her safe...How are you, sweetheart?"

Chapter Nineteen

"Y OU CAME!" CORI YANKED me inside. Her house was cool and airy, a great relief from the late June heat accumulating outside.

It was pool party day, the first day of summer vacation, the day I decided to make things right.

"I got your messages so I figured I'd better."

She'd left them on my home phone after my cell apparently went unanswered. Three messages, to be exact: one giving me the low down on the Lainey situation; the second asking if I'd forgive her for ever being Lainey's friend in the first place; and the third promising to fireman-carry me to her party if I wasn't there by eleven. I thought it would be a good idea to avoid giving Cori a hernia, so there I was, standing at her front door, wondering if it was too late to make up for all the lies I'd told her.

Cori's mother breezed into the entry from the kitchen and wrapped me in a hug.

"Jade, honey. It's been too long. How's your dad?" I

dissolved into her arms and breathed in the sweet scent of vanilla frosting from her apron.

When would Mom ever be able to stand in the front entry like this and greet my friends?

Soon. I had to keep believing it would be soon.

"Dad's good." Better than good, especially after talking to Mom until the battery on my cell ran out the night before.

"Well, tell him we say hi. We'd love to have you both over for a barbecue."

"Thanks, Mrs. Blake. He'd like that a lot." I smiled.

"Don't hog her, Mom," Cori joked and hustled me up the stairs.

We reached her bedroom, a haven of draping fabrics, beads, and scarves.

I dumped my backpack on her bed. "I wasn't sure you'd want me to come. I've been such a jerk lately."

Cori shut the door with a soft whoosh, then led me to her window seat and sat me down.

"So you're not mad at me?" Cori asked. "About the Lainey thing?"

"Of course not." I rubbed her arm and remembered how she'd stood up for me. "I'm the one who hasn't been much of a friend lately. Things have just been a bit nuts."

"This is about your mom, isn't it?" She stared, searching my face.

My mind raced. How could she know? Was Cori some kind of telepathic unicorn-girl or something? Given *my* secret identity, it was definitely within the realm of possibility. Or, maybe this was just the right time for me to spill.

"Well…yeah…it's about my mom…"

"I knew it! It was that Michaela bathing suit at Hyde's that started this, wasn't it? Darn it! I thought planning a pool party for you would be a good idea after the cruddy summer you had last year, but all it did was freak you out. I'm so sorry."

"You planned this for me?" I asked.

"Stupid, right?" Cori's mouth twisted into a hopeless expression.

"No, no! Not stupid at all. It's just…" I thought of the chain events that followed from that one simple bathing suit purchase, bringing us to here…

"What?" Cori asked.

How could I be honest about everything when I'd made that promise to Dad? But Cori deserved the truth. If we were going to stay best friends, I had to be one hundred percent completely honest. At least, as much as I *could* be.

"It's just that I found out something about the way my mom drowned, but I made a promise to my dad to keep the news within the family." It wasn't the whole truth, but it wasn't a lie. And it felt good. "That's why I've been acting so weird."

"Ohmigod!" Cori brought a hand to her mouth. "Did your mom commit suicide?" She pulled her hand away and whispered. "Was she…murdered?"

I laughed. "No, nothing like that. And I know it's not fair to you, but that's all I can say for now."

Cori seemed to process what I'd just said. "Okay. If you're asking me to chill, I will. But you know I'm going to be obsessing over this until I figure it out."

"Trust me. You wouldn't believe me if I told you." The words left my mouth and stirred a memory in me that I couldn't quite place.

"So, we're okay?" Cori asked.

"Definitely okay." I sighed and collapsed onto the big overstuffed cushions leaning against Cori's window seat. "As long as you're cool with me not swimming at your first-ever pool party."

"Why?" Cori asked.

"Well, if you do the math, the Super Sonic Slurpee Napkin Fiasco was about 28 days ago."

Cori understood. She took me by the shoulders and marched me to her en suite bathroom.

"Don't worry. We have the technology for that."

"It says Toxic Shock Syndrome can result in serious injury or death. Should I be worried about that?" I stuffed the instructions back into the tampon box.

Cori yelled through the closed door, "Come on, Jade! If you're done, get out here. Everyone's gonna be here soon!"

I got myself into my tankini, (after a quick side trip to the mall that morning to replace the bottoms), slathered on some SPF 40, and finished off the ensemble with the cutest thongs.

Flip-flops that is, not the butt cracking kind.

"Voilà!" I emerged from the bathroom. Cori nodded her head in approval.

"Looking good!"

"You look awesome too!" Cori was a knockout in her two-piece halter suit.

Slamming car doors sounded from outside, marking the arrival of guests. We kneeled over the window seat to get a peek outside. Kids were already streaming through the gate to the backyard.

"Looks like the party is about to start." Cori took me by the arm and giggled. "We shouldn't keep our guests waiting."

We hurried down the spiral staircase and crossed the main floor to the back of the house.

I stepped out onto the pool deck, welcoming the warm sun against my skin. My hair fell in waves against my bare shoulders, tickling them with stray tendrils. The heat from the sun brought out the scent of coconut from my sunscreen.

Ah…summer…

Everything about that moment made me almost believe that this might be my best summer, ever. And judging by the streamers and balloons, Cori was doing her best to kick it off to a good start.

"You really went all out, didn't you?" I whispered to Cori.

"Well you *are* a whole year older, after all."

"Wha…?"

Cori raised her hands like a cheerleader riling up a crowd.

"Happy Birthday!!!" everyone said at once.

Someone should have shot me with a clue gun, because it took a full minute before I registered what was going on.

"*My* birthday?" I stammered.

Cori laughed out loud. "You didn't think we were going to let your fourteenth birthday pass without celebrating?"

Then I remembered. So much had happened in the past month, I'd forgotten about my birthday in a few days.

"I got you a prezzie." Cori turned me around. When I looked up, there he was.

Luke closed the gate and rubbed his hands up and down the sides of his jeans, looking shy and adorable.

"Luke is my present?" I turned to Cori and hid my face. Why would he even want to be here after I ditched him the day before? I peeked long enough to see one of his friends nab him in conversation, buying me some time. "How did you get him to come?"

"I just called him. You like?" Cori whispered in my ear. "I finally clued in to why you'd developed such a habit of crashing into him. Plus, it wasn't totally selfless on my part." Cori looked past my shoulder and waved to Trey.

"Aw, Cori. You're the best." I smiled and gave her a huge bear hug.

"Well, don't just stand here. Go play with your present." Cori pushed me toward Luke and joined Trey by the pool.

"Luke," I called out. "Hey."

Luke's curls fell over his eyes when he turned. I thought I noticed him sigh as he made his way over. A horrible thought crossed my mind. Was he just doing Cori a favor?

"Hey, Jade. I hope it's okay that I'm here."

I tried to stay cool, but my whole body hummed at the sound of his voice.

"It's more than okay," I said, hoping that sigh meant nothing. Maybe it was just gas. Even gas would be better than a sigh. "I'm sorry I didn't make it to your boat cruise."

Luke seemed to choose his words. "I'm sure you were there in spirit."

Well, to be fair, I *was* there, just not exactly the way he might have imagined.

"Oh." Luke presented me with a brown paper bag. "Happy birthday."

"Thanks!" I took the bag from him.

"Sorry it's not much. I didn't have a lot of time with my cousin visiting and all. I didn't even get a chance to get my bathing suit."

"That's okay. I probably won't swim either." I wasn't quite ready to test the tampon theory, but Luke didn't have to know that. "But, really, you didn't have to get me anything."

He laughed. "Don't get your hopes up too much."

I peered into the crumpled paper bag. Wigwags. I smiled.

"Grandpa said you might like them." He winced. "Did I get it all wrong?"

"No, no. They're perfect. You really know the way to a

girl's heart." As soon as the words left my mouth, I inserted my foot. "Well, not my heart, my stomach, I mean." Then I thought of my muffin top and how I didn't particularly want a cute boy thinking about my stomach. "You know what I mean."

"They're my favorite too." Luke fished a Wigwag out of the bag and popped it in his mouth.

"Hey, those are *mine* now!" I slapped his hand away and laughed. We sat on the pool deck and I sloshed my feet in the water.

Cori strolled by with Trey on the way to the snack table.

"Aren't salt water pools great?" Cori asked. "Mom says her skin's never felt so soft."

I snatched my feet away. "Ah, um. A salt water pool, huh? That's, er, great!" I knew nothing would happen unless I actually dove in, but I pulled a towel over my legs and feet anyway and smiled.

Luke turned to me. "What's the matter?"

I plastered a smile on my face. "Oh, it's this weird foot thing. Just a little paranoid about the freaky toe structure I inherited from my mom."

"I've seen your toes before." Luke nudged me with his elbow.

I looked at him, trying to sort out what he'd just said. "You have?"

"That day at Bridget's, when I crushed your foot with my skateboard."

Luke had seen my toes. What did that mean?

He looked at me for a long moment. "You were wearing a blue hoodie."

Cue increased heart rate, dilating pupils, sweaty palms... "How do you remember that?" I gasped.

"You're kind of hard to forget, Jade." Luke looked down at his hands.

My brain clicked through our conversation like one of those plastic number games you get from the dollar store.

The hoodie.

My toes.

Bridget's.

"You went back to Bridget's to get your cell phone that day, didn't you?" I asked.

You push the little squares up, over and down, trying to get the numbers to line up from one to ten.

"Yeah." Luke stared into the pool.

"But you didn't go back to the skate park right away, did you?"

Luke stayed silent.

I tried to arrange my thoughts like the numbers in the game. Did Bridget tell Luke I was eating my lunch by the lake? Had he gone looking for me? Did he find me by the creek and cover me with the hoodie? I remembered the warning look Trey had given him when they returned to Bridget's later that afternoon. Had Luke told Trey what he'd seen? Was Trey in on it too?

"Luke." I worked to figure out a way to phrase my question without giving anything away. What if it really *was* Eddie who covered me up and not Luke? What if I was about to make a total idiot of myself? "Did something happen that day that changed the way you feel about me?"

"Listen, Jade…" Luke seemed to weigh his words. Maybe he thought I was trying to get him to say that he liked me. If I was way off and he knew nothing about me being a mermaid, he was probably trying to find a way to let me down easy.

But I'd said too much to go back now. "Did you see anything that day? Something you'd like to talk about?"

Luke took a deep breath, pulled off a shoe and held his foot in his hand. He leaned over.

You mean like this? The ring of his voice in my ear robbed my breath.

I blinked. My mouth hung open. He had the same webbed toes as I did.

It *was* him.

He pulled the hoodie over me that day, next to the creek. He'd seen me in my half-mermaid phase and knew exactly what it meant. Because…he was a mer too.

Yes, I rang back, *exactly like that.*

"What's that ringing sound?" Cori squinted and glanced around as she pulled Trey toward us. "Is that someone's cell phone?"

I'm not sure what came over me, call it temporary insanity or any of Dr. Becker's other diagnoses, but I was so stunned by what had just happened and so surprised when

Cori broke into our conversation that I grabbed Luke around the neck and kissed him.

On the lips.

"Ohh-kay…" Cori giggled. "We'll just be over *there* if you need us."

Finally, long after Cori left, purely to make sure it was safe to talk again, I let the poor boy go.

"Sorry about that," I said breathlessly.

Luke smiled his adorable curvy smile. "I thought we were going to stop apologizing to each other."

"Right. Sorry."

"You're doing it again." He laughed.

My hand flew to my mouth to stifle one of my signature snorts. Then, I pulled it away and stared at him, trying to make sense of what was happening.

*So you're a…*I switched back to my mermaid voice but could barely form the words.

Luke nodded.

But how? Is Eddy…is the rest of your family?

Luke laughed and shook his head. *No. I'm, um…I guess you would call it adopted.* He brought his hand up to the side of my face and tucked a strand of hair behind my ear.

"Oh…" I think I muttered. Though, I couldn't think. Not with his hand so close to my cheek and his eyes holding my gaze.

The earth seemed to tilt back on its axis and set itself right again. Mom was back in the ocean on her way to becoming human, Cori was the best friend a girl could ever have, and I was sitting next to a boy who knew all my deepest, darkest secrets and didn't seem to mind. He was a merman or a Pesco-boy or whatever, and I could almost imagine what that all meant and in the same second, I couldn't wrap my head around it at all.

But then, that all fell away, because he kissed me back.

The kiss took every full body collision, misuse of pronouns, and curvy-lipped smile and mixed them up with the chocolaty-caramel-goodness of the last Wigwag in the box. Add Luke's impossibly soft lips, his hand in my hair, and his warm breath on my face, and you would still only be partway there.

Because the kiss was made of awesome.

"Luke?" I asked.

"Yeah?"

"Does this mean you'll stop knocking me over every time you want to say hello?"

He laughed and kissed me again.

And that definitely registered on a boy-girl level.

In a major, big time way.

Jade's 5-minute Chocolate Mug Cake

---

*When Wigwags are in short supply, this is the
quickest way I've found to chocolate bliss.*

First, get yourself the biggest microwaveable mug in the
cupboard. In it put:

- 4 tablespoons flour
- 4 tablespoons sugar
- 2 tablespoons cocoa

Mix it well. Then add:

- 1 egg

Mix. Then add:

- 3 tablespoons milk
- 3 tablespoons oil

Mix. Then add:

- 3 tablespoons chocolate chips (NOT optional—at least
  as far as I'm concerned)
- 1 capful of vanilla extract

And…wait for it…MIX!

Cook for 3 minutes at 1000 watts (high). The cake will look like it's going to overflow but don't freak out!

Let it cool for a bit (unless you want to burn your lips off) then ENJOY!

NOTES & TIPS:

Some say this can serve 2 but, yeah right; whatever.

TAKE OUT THE SPOON before you microwave the mug. Don't ask me why I know this...

CAN YOU BELIEVE IT?

With this recipe, you are only ever 5 minutes away from chocolate bliss! You're going to make this RIGHT NOW, aren't you?

Jade

Acknowledgments

Writing a book is a lot like wrestling a giant squid, but it is a process made much easier with the help of keen-eyed critical readers, including my wonderful Kidcrit pals and super-patient friends and family.

Much thanks to my agent, Lauren MacLeod, for fishing me out of her slush pile and for navigating me through all of my writerly efforts. Thanks also to my editor, Rebecca Frazer, who jumped in with both feet and helped me tell this tale as authentically as possible.

Marcelle, Charlotte, and Gord: you are my constant sources of support and inspiration. None of this happens without you.

About the Author

Hélène Boudreau writes fiction and non-fiction for children and young adults from her landlocked home in Ontario, Canada, though she grew up on an island surrounded by the Atlantic Ocean. She has never spotted a mermaid in the wild but believes they are just as plausible as sea horses, flying fish, or electric eels. Her debut middle grade novel, *Acadian Star*, was nominated for the 2009–2010 Hackmatack Children's Choice Book Award. You can visit her at: www.heleneboudreau.com.